The LAST NARROW GAUGE TRAIN ROBBERY

By Robert K. Swisher, Jr.

Sunstone Press
Santa Fe, New Mexico

For Moose, who rode those mountain trails,
drank that rot gut whiskey;
sometimes old friend, you have to bite the bullet . . . .

Printed in the United States of America

Library of Congress Cataloging in Publication Data

Swisher, Robert K., 1947-
    The last narrow gauge train robbery.

    I. Title.
PS3569.W574L37   1987   813'.54   87-6491
ISBN: 0-86534-106-0

Published in 1987 by SUNSTONE PRESS
            Post Office Box 2321
            Santa Fe, NM 87504-2321 / USA

CHAPTER 1

With each passing mile, Bill Masterson felt the tension drain from his body. Another thirty minutes and he would be on the edge of the mountains; another year, another yearly trip. God, the time flew anymore. He wondered if they would make it. He prayed they would. This would make the tenth year and nobody had missed yet; but, the apprehension was always there. Although they were all in their mid-thirties, one day somebody would be the first to die. What shit life is, Bill decided. He rummaged around in his shirt pocket and dug out the inch-long roach of Afghani weed. As the smoke curled around his head, Bill once again fell back into the joy of not thinking about responsibilities, and picturing the mountain trail that would lead his friends and him high into the San Juan Wilderness to Green Lake.

At the edge of the mountains, Bill drove toward Chama. Surrounded by the Santa Fe Forest and the San Juan Wilderness, the New Mexico town is the kickoff point for many different people wishing to see a glimpse of an America that is rapidly shrinking. During the summer, an endless line of bird watchers, fishermen, and campers make their way through the town. During the fall, grouse, elk, deer, and big horn sheep hunters fill the woods.

Chama consists of people who don't want to ask questions and don't want to answer any. Six bars line the main street, scratching out a living from truck drivers trying to dodge scales and outdoorsmen. The only establishment that makes a good living year round is the Wagon Wheel Bar because the owner, a Mr. Saavedra, loves girls with big tits, dreams of girls with big tits, only hires girls with big tits. With big tits ingrained in modern society, the Wagon Wheel always has enough men in it to pay the bills.

Years earlier, Bill Masterson had heard about the bar on the C.B. as he was driving north of Albuquerque.

"Lord," the trucker had said, "her tits were the best I've seen in years. Big enough to get your tongue hard."

After that, the yearly meeting place before the onslaught into the wilderness was changed to the Wagon Wheel. After all, the thinking was, if a group of has-been hippies was going to meet once a year from all corners of the country to go fishing, they might as well meet at a place where the barmaids have big tits.

Scattered behind the bar are several hundred small wooden homes which look like they belong more in the midwest than New Mexico. At this elevation, there are no quaint adobe homes selling for ridiculous prices. Instead, wood frame homes sell for ridiculous prices.

At one time, the staff of life to the town was the lumber mill. One either worked at the mill, cut the trees in the forest, or drove the trucks that hauled the trees. But, when the mill played out, it was the narrow gauge railroad that came to the rescue. Now, the small town is mostly known for its potatoes and the hookers who come from nowhere during the hunting season.

Before the fall of the wood mill, the narrow gauge had consisted of nothing but rotting passenger cars and two old broken steam engines. The old tracks were torn and twisted. Two men from Texas, just out of the woods from hunting elk, were sitting in the Wagon Wheel enjoying the tits and getting drunk when one turned to the other.

"I bet I can take that old railroad and make it into a money maker."

The other Texan took a big pull on his beer and laughed. "You're nuts, five thousand dollars says you'll loose your ass."

People laughed when the word got around . . . at first. But when crews came in and fixed the forty-some miles of track, rebuilt the tiny steam-powered engine, and refurbished the wooden open-air passenger cars, people didn't snicker as much. Then, the first year when a lot of people came to ride the train, many people began to say, "Maybe it will make some money." But the following year when Willie Nelson rode the train, everybody knew that money was coming to town. Everybody was in a rush to come out with the first Narrow Gauge T-shirts and other assorted gear that comes with success.

And money did come. Texas money, Iowa money, everybody with their sweaters and cameras and walking shorts and squeaking leather boots came. Came to sit for five hours and watch the mountains roll by while being banged and bounced along the tiny narrow gauge tracks.

It is a beautiful ride, a fantasy for the overworked and misplaced people of our country. It is a culture shock. There are no buildings, no coke stands along the way, no cops, no stop signs. Only the wind and trees, grouse and jays, wild canaries, deer and elk, a few disgruntled bear holding tenaciously to a last small primitive area of the state, and the small, coal-powered engine, the last of its kind, taking remnants of humanoids over the mountains.

On some days the sun shines, and the mountains simmer in the sun. On most days during the summer, the mountains rest with the clouds, and the trees and canyons peek at you as if trying to hide as you clink by. All in all, most people like the ride. Taking two to three rolls of film, oohing and ahhing at the scenery around them, engrossed but a little afraid. What if the train breaks, what if they have to sleep in the woods? But there was never a what if, only the chug, chug of the little train. The train brought back life, filled with tourists. No great hulks of miners, no Indians, no gunfighters or outlaws filling the cars. No men looking for a new life, gold or silver. No men out to settle a country. Just men and women, trapped men and women, pulling little kids with suckers while their cameras bounce around their necks.

To Bill Masterson and his friends, Chama was a place; a collection of years and laughter, or telling old jokes and laughing at each other. Of getting drunk in the Wagon Wheel and looking at the tits. It was a fantasy lived out each year. A meeting of old anti-establishment hippies, too old, too tired, too filled with families and responsibilities to fight on; but, still brave enough for a week once a year to dream and laugh with old crazy friends and talk about things they would never do but always wanted to. They would meet and laugh and go to the mountains for their week, and then they would part and go back to their world away from the mountains and Chama. Leave to remember the trout they caught and the elk they saw and the puff of smoke the Narrow Gauge left as it pulled out of town. And each in his truck would feel sad, each alone, each going a different direction. But there would be another year. For a year they would dream of the next fishing trip. It was a staff, a caring bond with a part of mankind. It was like rock and fire and the wind, solid, life-giving. It was a reason in this life- shattering, demoralizing, rat race world, to be alive.

Bill Masterson stopped the pickup on the outskirts of town and got out. The yellow Ford was spotless. The green two-horse trailer stood out from the truck. Bill walked back and looked into the trailer. The two horses pawed and snorted while pee flowed onto the highway. The truck cost nothing sitting next to the car all year. Washed and vacuumed, its only function was to remain washed and vacuumed for

5

this one ride to the mountains. About the truck he heard very little from his wife. But the horses, eighty bucks a month for each one to eat and shit. "Jesus," his wife would say when the kids were in bed, "all they do is eat and shit, eat and shit, and once a year carry your camping gear up into the mountains to see your old hippie friends." Bill had heard it so many times that he said nothing, until one day. One winter, while patting Slick's head, she said it. He turned calmly, looked at her squinted eyes, and spoke, "If you don't like it, get a job." From that day on, nothing was said about the yellow truck, the green horse trailer, or the two glue bags he loved so dearly.

Bill breathed deep the clean mountain air. Down the street he could see the Wagon Wheel bar. His heart thumped loudly in his chest as he walked towards the bar. Dear God, he thought, let everybody be here.

Standing at the door, he noticed immediately that Saavedra must still own the bar. Two women with huge tits lazed behind the counter. They smiled at him as he sat down. He ordered a draft and wondered how he could possibly get the barmaids to take off their blouses. Watching the girl walk away from the bar, he chuckled to himself. There were a lot of years between hippie and father of four, between freedom and working for the Fire Department. He gazed into his beer. He felt good. For a period of time, there would be nothing to bother his mind.

He looked at the waitress and raised his glass for another one. He had made it. The other barmaid started toward him with his beer. Bill studied closely the outline of her nipples, an old adage he always remembered, women with big nipples get turned on more than girls with small ones. The girl smiled without inhibition, she knew her tits kept her employed. Resting her tits on the bar, she grinned once more before walking back to talk to her friend. Bill rubbed his face, took several deep breaths, and thought of his wife. The more he thought, the more he wanted to sleep with the barmaid. She was, indeed, the hottest thing he had seen in months or at least since the cute young blonde he had pulled out of the burning apartment wearing nothing but a dark nightgown and crotchless panties. Even during a fire one could appreciate good pussy.

Bill sipped his beer and waited for the others. He turned in the chair and looked out the window. It was dark now, and the gold Miller sign made his reflection bounce back from the window. What he saw didn't make him unhappy. With his square shoulders, dark hair, and neatly trimmed mustache, he was still good-looking. His hair didn't recede and he still pissed with vigor. But inside he was tired. Lord, here he was, grabbing his time like his father — raising kids, playing it so straight, smiling and talking when talked to — wanting to do anything besides be a fireman in Albuquerque. All in all, there were worse things in life than having been unable to beat the system. He knew one thing. The longer one fucked with the man, the better his chances were of going to jail. It was a lot easier to be bored than brave. He turned from the window and sipped his beer. Down the street the Narrow Gauge engine blew off excess steam before shutting down for the night. The shrill sound echoed through the town, sounding alone and lost.

CHAPTER 2

Ronnie Wild pulled the jeep pickup into the parking lot of the Wagon Wheel. The back of the truck was filled with his fishing gear and the food. Last year he had inherited next year's food list. He stepped out of the truck and stretched. It was a long drive from Los Angeles to Chama, but it was good. Each year the difference between the two seemed greater. After the lights and noise and hustle of LA, Chama was almost not breathing. But God it was good. Each year he would see the edge of Chama and remember the small cabin he had lived in.

It was here they had met, all of them, the group. He had come out with his girl right off the streets of 'Frisco, flying on any item that was supposed to enhance your life, groove your mind, or get you fucked up. The mountains around Chama taught him life. Snow was cold, work was a part of life. Just because one stayed stoned and grooved on nature did not mean that one did not have to eat and, most important, just because a pregnancy might result didn't mean that one had to forego the pleasure of screwing.

After two winters and two summers he had dragged himself back to LA, let his mother hug him, put up his hippie flower-child bride and baby, and went back to college. In time, he had his law school degree. But he never forgot the mountains. No matter what case he was working on, no matter what the trouble, he could move his thoughts to the sound of the old wood stove and the breathtaking sight of the stars at night, and relax. The mountains were always close to Ronnie. There were many times when he felt like leaving his home, his Jaguar, his Mercedes, his kids with their motorbikes and surfboards, and returning to the mountains. But he never did. He settled for this week, his week with the old guys, converted like him.

Ronnie walked into the bar and saw the back of Bill's head. He sat down without speaking and looked at his old friend. Bill smiled and the two men looked at each other. After a few moments, they shook hands. Bill waved for another beer.

"I'm glad you're not dead," Bill toasted. Their glasses clanked and they chugged the beer. Both laughed, stood, and hugged each other.

"How are the kids?" Bill asked.

Ronnie chuckled, "One smokes pot, but not like us. He just does it . . . you know. When we started, it was a cause, something, remember?"

Bill agreed silently.

"One kid likes pills and the other is going to grow up and make a bundle selling coke."

Bill laughed, "Sounds like my crew. I tell the oldest, if he thinks he can get ahead selling drugs, he better think about it." Bill leaned closer to Ronnie, "But if he does, I'll let him build up, then I'll rip him off myself, and retire up here." Both men laughed.

"No, seriously," Ronnie continued, "kids are fine, good kids. They would never guess that we used to live up here, smoke grass and live off the land."

Both men kept their thoughts hidden. Life had been so easy back then, so simple. It was only a matter of where your head was that made the world. The lesson had been well-learned, though, never to be forgotten. The world was bigger than they were. Their peckers had, indeed, gotten them in trouble.

"How is the fire business?" Ronnie asked.

"Jesus," Bill spoke, "let me tell you about the blonde I pulled out of an apartment with the crotchless panties. Finger lickin' good."

Ronnie moved his hand for two more beers. "I see Saavedra still owns the bar. I wonder where he finds these girls." Ronnie watched the tits of the barmaid as they bounced toward them. "What they need is a wet T-shirt night.''

"What they really need is herpes, like California,'' Bill laughed.

For a few moments they said nothing. Both were content as they realized how fast the year had passed. Another year, a year that seemed like nothing. It was funny, everything except the mountains, the fishing, and the trip seemed to be the dream of their lives. It made no sense.

Bill poked Ronnie with his elbow, "I have some Afghani that will do the trick this year.''

Ronnie rolled his eyes back, "Good, I have some coke that is at least sixty percent mannitol.'' Both men laughed and took another slug of beer.

"God, it's good to see you,'' Ronnie spoke.

At that moment, Riley Page entered the bar, all five feet eight inches of him. Dressed in Levis and a western shirt, he looked like a short version of the Marlboro Man. When they had first met, Riley was fresh out of Vietnam. The first year he lived in the mountains, he couldn't get it up unless the girl put on a camouflage T-shirt. He was plagued with recurring dreams that it was all built on the side, and a constant fear that he would develop syphilis when he was old.

Both Ronnie and Bill jumped up, and the three men danced in a small circle. They began to chant — big tits — big tits — big tits. The bar girls smiled and brought them a round of beer. During the greeting, two cowboys came into the bar and sat at the far end. Both looked tired, smelled of cow shit, and looked like yesterday's windstorm. Ronnie, Bill, and Riley paid them no mind. There was nobody in their world, only them, the beer, and the big tits on the bar girls.

"Fuckin' Saavedra still finds 'em,'' Riley spoke, spilling beer down his chin. After the hippie phase of his life, Riley had gone back to school and received a degree in photography. He got a job teaching at the University in Denver and spent his time fucking young college girls. He still was not married.

"Listen,'' he would say, "you can have your kids, your wives, your responsibility. No steady squeeze for this kid. I'll take my chances getting herpes.''

There was nothing finer to Riley than the beginning of the new school year, and the anticipation of which young coed would be sitting in the front row. He counted beavers like some people counted the fish they caught. But the highlight of each year was this week in the mountains. Whatever else Riley was, he loved the mountains.

The dreamer, the veteran, the photographer. He was constantly on the search to make life more than it was.

The three men sat at the bar. By nine there were over half-a-dozen other customers staring at the girls through the cloud of cigarette smoke.

Riley looked out the window into the darkness. "Frank is usually here by now," he spoke to himself more than to the others.

Everyone looked nervously at each other until Bill told a joke, "You heard about the new DeLorean car? You drive around the street until the white lines disappear."

"That reminds me, anybody want a toot?" Ronnie asked, not laughing. Riley nooded his head and took the folded paper as Ronnie handed it to him under the bar.

As Riley walked off, Ronnie looked at Bill, "You know, the bathroom has become, in modern times, the most active area of any party or restaurant. Have you noticed how many people go to the bathroom with somebody else?"

Bill scratched his head, "I wonder what will be next on the list of recreational drugs that blow your mind."

Ronnie sipped his beer, "I don't know, but whatever it is, I hope a lot of it grows in my back yard."

Riley walked by the assorted cowboys and Mexicans along the bar. Inside the bathroom, he locked the door and opened the folded wrapper. Taking his knife from his belt, he dipped the point in the white powder and placed it under his nose. He inhaled, made a face, and repeated the process. He folded the paper carefully and went back to the bar. Sitting back down by Ronnie, he slipped the paper back to him.

"Jesus, you buy the worst shit I have ever snorted. That must be at least sixty percent mannitol."

Ronnie shook his head, "That's what I figured."

Bill put his hand under the bar, "Let me have some of that shit."

Bill made his way past the line of onlooking Mexicans and cowboys. One nodded, one smirked, and one drank his beer. Inside the bathroom, Bill opened the paper carefully, poked his finger in the pile, and then rubbed his gums. He had heard that this was better, no chance of burning holes in your nose. Walking back past the line of beer drinkers, nobody looked.

After he sat down, he handed the paper back to Ronnie, "Riley is right," he spoke, "that stuff is terrible."

"Sugar rush better than no rush," Ronnie chirped.

By ten in the evening, all the men were sufficiently full of beer to make the walk to the bathroom after each glass. Filled with mannitol, the beer didn't seem to have any effect except to run through their bodies, leaving nothing but a few hops and grain as it went.

"You know," Bill spoke, "I know I've pissed a fortune in my life; enough beer to fill a beer truck, buy a house in the mountains, do a drug deal."

Everybody laughed. Riley sat drinking his beer and became silent while Bill and Ronnie told stories. Bill noticed his quietness, "Now don't go getting sentimental on us yet, Riley."

Riley was known to grow despondent. His attacks would come at various times, eating, drinking, driving, sitting in the tent with the guys, in the middle of making love. Riley had a general and precise understanding of the futility of the human condition. At times, there was not enough outside stimulus to keep the wisdom covered, and he would see everything as the passing thing it is.

He looked at Bill and Ronnie, "We're just like all the rest," he spoke quietly, "cramming moments and periods of time we love into small bits of life. Hung up, strung up, fucked up; God, how depressing to be lumped in with mankind."

Bill sipped his beer as Riley continued. "Remember when we first met — sitting in our log homes, cutting wood, freezing our asses — boy did we know the world. We believed we were the changers of life, everybody would join the flock. Remember sitting and smoking pot, discussing life and love, war, hate? Now look at us, scattered across the face of America. We fit. We molded our thoughts and beliefs until we fit." Riley started to continue, but Bill cut in.

"Everybody had to fit, everybody has to, Riley. Nobody here is a hermit, nobody can keep the vigil. Fuckin' world is too big. We were just like everything else, a passing, that's how it is. Nobody likes it, but that's how it is."

Riley looked at Bill, looked at Ronnie, sipped his beer. "I know," he spoke with a twinkle in his eye. "I know, but what a bummer."

Ronnie chuckled, "You ex-hippie fuck. Maybe you should go back to living off the land or sell a load of pot."

Riley scratched his ear, "No, that's over. Used to be a bunch of guys sold pot, heros, culture heros, not now. Italians, Cubans, and Colombians now, big fat grease balls with diamonds and fancy cars, and people who will cut your fingers off and kill your mother.

11

Gangsters, nothing but gangsters. You know, it's like everything else, too many people, too popular. If you have good thing going, keep it small and quiet."

One of the big-titted barmaids walked down in front of them smiling. Riley lost his melancholy look as he stared at the tits before him.

The girl looked at Riley. He pushed a ten dollar bill in front of the girl and spoke, "Ten bucks and let me see your tits."

The girl didn't stop smiling, but leaned forward and whispered, "See that man at the end of the bar?"

"Yes," Riley answered, "the big guy with the nose that looks like it caught too many fists?"

"That is my husband," the girl answered.

Riley smiled, "Ten dollars to keep your mouth shut."

The girl laughed and slipped the ten dollars in her cleavage.

Ronnie chuckled, "This isn't your freshman photography class here."

Riley shivered, "Give me that wrapper, I need another toot."

Frank Cummings felt the four horses moving in the trailer. He scratched his balding head and sipped on the Coors beer. In the back of the truck was all the gear, tents, packsaddles, fishing poles. Every year, he brought the pack gear and the four horses. Of all the men, he still lived in the mountains. He had become a guide and outfitter, hanging on to his dream of freedom. Somehow, he had managed to stay alive during the lean years. By growing a few pot plants, he always seemed to make it. While the others were getting their ladies pregnant, he was like Riley.

"No sir, not me," he swore. And he went down and had the knots put in. It wasn't that he didn't like kids, he just figured that if the world was as fucked up as it was, why have more people to make it more fucked up?

"After the war is when we'll need more kids," he told everybody, "but not mine. I'd hate for people to walk around with my brain."

During the year he never went to see Bill in Albuquerque, even though he was only a hundred miles away. Frank was the kind of guy who loved his friends dearly, but after a week, people made him nervous. He would have to run back to his cabin and sit alone and relax. There were periods in his life when he could only sleep with a gun by the bed, one behind the door, one in each drawer he might open, and one in his back pocket. To most people, Frank was distant, quiet, not easy to understand or get to know. Handsome in a cowboy way, he was a loner, a man who sat and watched the world from his hermit hideaway. To Frank, life boiled down to his favorite phrase, cocksuckers; everything, everybody, at one time or another, was a cocksucker. Horses were cocksuckers, trees, chainsaws, trucks, doors, radios, presidents, kings, mailmen, tax men, and people in general. Frank finished the warm beer in his hand and parked the truck across the street from the Wagon Wheel. He could see the reflections of his three friends behind the Miller sign. He took some hay from the truck, fed the horses, and walked toward the bar.

Entering the bar, he looked at the backs of the heads of his companions. The various people in the bar were all involved in some overly loud conversation about something the government was doing to fuck it all up.

Frank walked up behind Bill, Riley and Ronnie and hollered, "Cocksuckers." The three men jerked around, relief flooding their faces.

"Jesus Christ," Ronnie blurted out, "we were getting worried."

"Won't be me the first to die," Frank laughed, "only the good die young."

The four men sat and were silent for a moment. Frank got his beer and looked at the others. He stood.

"A toast to ex-hippies and dreamers and outlaws at large." He raised his voice and looked at the other men in the bar and hollered, "Fuck the communist cocksuckers." The various people responded with grunts and scowls.

At mignight they decided it was time to go. Bill left the bar first. Outside, the stars seemed as though they could be touched. Bill stood and saw the Narrow Gauge train resting silently with the night. Bill saw what looked like the engineer climb down from the engine. For a moment, it was as though the man with the bib overalls and the train silhouetted behind him were pulled out of place and made one entity. The train seemed to twist and turn until the headlight was following the old man and it watched him until he walked into a small house by the tracks. Bill looked at the train and the space where the man had been. He began to wave his arms and make strange noises. When the others came out of the bar, he was standing there looking crazed.

They looked at him. "What is it? What is it?" Ronnie asked.

Bill shook his hands and looked at the stars. "I know what it is," he hollered, "I know what it all is."

"What is it?" Frank asked.

Bill put this hands down and lowered his voice, "There's not enough outlaws left; do you understand, there's not enough outlaws left."

Bill turned and looked at the train, then turned and looked at his friends once again. For a moment, he was lonely; for his friends, for the train, for the old man. He didn't know exactly why, but he was lonely.

Leaving two vehicles parked by the bar, Frank and Ronnie unloaded Ronnie's gear and got into Frank's truck. Bill and Riley got into the other. Pulling the horse trailers behind, they started off in the dark, headlights reflecting off the trees and barbed wire fences that bordered the highway. Frank stared into the dark. It seemed so distant — the trees, the dark — so solid and impersonal, uncaring, filled with eons of time. And he was with it all, so small and tiny and vulnerable. They drove into the mountains, and stopped at the trail head to sleep. Around them the crickets chirped and the mountains waited.

CHAPTER 3

Matthew Crane rose before the alarm went off. He walked through the hall to the kitchen, lit the gas stove, and placed the already prepared coffee pot on the burner. Outside, it was still pitch black; but, within an hour, the sun would touch the trees by the river, turning their dark forms crimson.

He walked to the bathroom and washed his face. It was not a bad face for seventy-two years, what you could see of it. All one could really make out were the piercing, captivating blue eyes that looked out upon the world from a circle of white curly hair and an out-of-control white beard. People called him Santa when he wasn't around. He washed his face, put his teeth from the jar by the sink in his mouth, and thanked God for another day. Back in the bedroom, he pulled on his grey-blue striped bib overalls and set the matching engineer's cap on his head. Walking back to the kitchen, he sat down, rolled a Bull Durham cigarette, and drank his coffee.

The sun began to turn the horizon red, and the chorus of morning dogs started across town. Matthew stood and began to move his large frame toward the door. Outside, the morning was chilly but comfortable. Matthew walked slowly, dragging his oil-stained boots. At the restaurant across the street, Grace would have his lunch ready. His life beat the hell out of sitting in the old folk's home back in Albuquerque. Matthew had a lot to be thankful for, and he treated people around him in that manner. He was friendly, helpful, and quiet in an old man sort of way.

Two years earlier, it had been another day at the home for Matthew. Another boring, starched, and clean antiseptic day. He had eaten his gruel, swallowed his toast, taken his pill, and drunk his juice, just like the young nurse with the nice round ass had told him to. He had then walked like the prisoner he was to the sun room and started to read the paper. It was the same very day except the days he didn't eat his gruel, or take his pill, or pinch the nurse's ass. It was the same until he saw the want ads:

"Wanted. Man with experience with narrow gauge steam engines."

An address was given with a time, "Apply in person." Matthew cut the ad out of the paper and the next day walked away from the home, or the pen, as he called it. It had been easy from there. There had been nobody else qualified for the job. The young man doing the hiring · looked worried until Matthew smiled at him and spoke, "Don't worry, I won't die driving the train. Put a young man on with me and I'll train him."

Two days later, Matthew was on the bus headed for Chama as chief engineer of the Narrow Gauge Railroad. It was a dream, a new world, a coming out, a rebirth. For Matthew, a railroad man for his entire life, it was the completion of a circle.

He was everywhere around the train, checking, looking, feeling, touching the black engine. In time, the engine became his, not a large cast iron hunk of steel, but his. His outdated, antique old engine, made to run by love and caring.

Matthew would stand and watch the people board the small passenger cars, the cars with their straight-backed red wooden seats.

And then he would climb into the open engine and lay on the steam. The engine would shake and bounce and groan and ever so slowly it would start, one inch, two inches, groaning, proving it could continue. One-tenth the size of a modern locomotive, but full of guts. And it would climb and wheeze up the treacherous 14,000 foot mountain with its switchbacks and upgrades and downgrades. All the time Matthew would talk to the engine. His old hands would be the steel wheels, his heart the steam boiler.

Soon, he was as famous as the train itself. His face was on postcards mailed around the world. Children asked him questions and sat in his chair, looking at the gauges and firebox. From early May until the last run in the winter, Matthew had not missed a day in two years. He was never sick. "Had all those fuckin' diseases," he would say, and didn't drink more than one beer a night. In time, the town grew to love him. It was forgotten that he hadn't been born there.

Matthew opened the door of the restaurant and looked at the short, thin, Mexican lady behind the counter. It was early, before the people and the rush; nice. There was time for a smile. Grace handed Matthew his lunch, courtesy of the railroad.

"Nice day," Matthew spoke.

"Nice day," Grace answered as she busied herself behind the counter. Through the months, they had become good friends. Both were alone, both felt a bond.

"Trees will start to change before long," Matthew spoke. "Thought I saw a few yellow aspen leaves yesterday."

Grace smiled, "Another year, they go fast."

Matthew looked at the lady and could think of nothing to say. "Well, time to get going."

The bell on the door clanged behind him. In the early light, he could see several men moving about the train. By ten, everything would be ready and the passengers would be boarding. He walked across the street and up to the engine. The engine was small, twenty feet long, its large cattle bumper reaching over the track. Behind the large, round, steam boiler, one had a few feet to stand or sit in front of the coal bin. All around the engine, one could smell the mixture of coal and steam and grease. Matthew loved this engine. There would be no world without it. With this train he could look back in time to see the mountains before the tourist, before the paved highway, to a time when the train was shiny and new. To a time when it was the only vehicle that climbed the mountain, carrying gold and silver out of the high passes. At times, Matthew could see the old-timers, the drummers and miners, the explorers and bad men. Sitting in the engine he could look back and see, standing by the passenger cars, men in leather and furs with large, well-oiled guns hanging from their hips and shoulders. There would be sheriffs hopping a ride to the top with their horses to hunt down bandits trying to hide in the vast, untamed wilderness. At times, he could see piles of hides and meat waiting for markets back East, and an occasional woman, all perfumed up with feathers in her hat, leaving a sordid past behind with the mountains.

Matthew knew the little train, the creaks and groans. He knew when it needed coal or water, knew when it needed grease and oil. The train talked to him and he listened. Both were in tune with time, and space, and dreams. Both were old and tired, but pertinent to a world that moved onward too quickly, too fast to enjoy or see unless moments were grabbed by cameras as one ran frantically through life. He stepped up into the engine, nodding to the apprentice engineer, touched the throttle, and laughed out loud, "Today, won't neither of us die." And he pulled the whistle that woke up the town.

CHAPTER 4

If one were to fly north from Chama, New Mexico, one would start at 7,000 feet and fly over the mountains looming up to 14,000. It is a green, lush land in the summer, dotted by fir and spruce and aspen stands. The high peaks and meadows pasture for sheep and cattle in the summer. In the winter it is white with snow. The land around the foothills of the mountains is divided, for the most part, into private ranches; big spreads boasting of times in the past when they made a living. Now ghosts of what they were, most are owned by oil men and sheiks who use them for tax write-offs and hunting. They run a few cows to help them feel like cowboys. The ranches are worked by young men, men with large drooping western hats, boots with their Levis tucked in the top, and spurs that ring when they walk. Dead men already, hanging onto a dream that died before them. They are but tokens on the ranches, living legends who, for a few years, will live their glory; sleeping with the young cowboy girls poured into their tight Levis, dreaming of six guns and cattle rustlers, reading their Louis L'Amour books until the day comes when they get one of the little cowgirls pregnant and move into a trailer, then rising each day to work in the mill or drive a truck.

The mountains that are excluded from the boundaries of the ranches are considered wilderness or natural forests. A huge tract of land running between Pagosa Springs and Durango on the west, and Chama and Antonito on the south and east remains relatively unspoiled. Left to the government, it will be spoiled. The trail heads are areas where one may start into the wilderness either on foot or horseback. Motorized vehicles are not allowed. In the lakes that dot the wilderness, brook and cut-throat trout leap into the air from the stillness of mirror-smooth water. The people who come to this country come to be alone or to be with friends. It is a small haven for the lost and disenchanted ones who come to be with the wind and the forest. It is a place to run to, to breathe the fresh air, and to see one's life.

Before the 1860s, there was nothing back in the wilderness except a few outlaws and a few Indians. By the 1870s, gold and silver had been discovered, and a rough-cut road circled up and through Grouse Mountain, Cumbres Pass, and Munga Pass, ending at the small mining community of Platoro. Here, miners worked for the large mining company until they had a grub stake, and could then head into the mountains to pan the streams and dig the outcroppings in search of their glory hole. The trails that came from these miners are the trails that people follow now, searching for quiet. It is a timeless place, a place where the seasons come and go without our help. A place where nature is alone most of the year, sealed by remoteness from our perils.

Snaking around the edge of this wilderness is the Narrow Gauge Railroad. Running partially by the super highway, it is a black, smoke-belching attraction that makes all the cars stop and look in wonder at a portion of our past. The train runs by the highway for ten miles before it cuts off into the forest, climbing over the passes to coast into Colorado. It is a living memory, a memory of gold and silver, guards with double-barreled shotguns riding with the cars, nervous, waiting for the sound of the rifle or crack of a pistol. Hanging in the office of the Narrow Gauge Railroad is an old, browned-out photograph of four men who tried to rob the Chama train. They are strung from a cottonwood tree by the river, their necks extended out past life, dreams of riches and no work gone forever. Standing around the four is a group of smiling men, their hats pulled over their eyes, their guns crossed in their arms. There is no date, there are no names. It was just another event in the mountains not worth remembering.

When the mine played out, and the rivers did not yield enough gold to warrant any more exploring, Platoro, Chama and the railroad died, slipped peacefully back into the seasons. A few crooks and ranchers stayed on, along with a few hermits. Not until the 1960s did the land wake up once again. Hippies, the disenchanted ones, moved in from all over the world, looking for peace and love and the truth. They found Mexicans who hated Anglos, cowboys who hated Mexicans and about everything else, including cold, and the truth. But they also found the wilderness. A wilderness not overrun like Yellowstone or Yosemite. And then, as if by magic, people began to remember the forest. People all over the country were filled with the fear it was ending. One day there would be only photographs. Elk and deer would be stuffed or in zoos, and people began to flock to the outback. It was here that Bill, Ronnie, Riley and Frank came every year, came to remember old times and old places, came to laugh at the days when they cut wood to heat their homes, and walked through the snow to the outhouse. They laughed about being stuck in the woods, carrying guns to scare off the Mexicans and cowboys who didn't like longhairs.

It is different now. People don't care about the hair. There are enough problems without worrying about someone's hair. Like the train, the gold, silver, and the big ranches, Frank, Riley, Bill, and Ronnie settled onto the shelf of antiquity. They settled their shoulders a little, and took life for what it was.

"It's a mind-fuck," Ronnie exclaimed.

"It's a cocksucker," Frank declared.

"It's a bunch of shit," Bill knew.

"It's a photograph of a rose-colored asshole," Riley observed.

CHAPTER 5

They all woke up at the same time with the morning sun streaming through the truck glass. By the wood corral built by the Forest Service, a meadowlark was singing. They stepped from the truck, stretching cramped muscles. Around them in every direction the mountains loomed, studded with granite and limestone bluffs. On each vista, the snow-capped peaks poked through the early morning clouds. Down an aspen-studded hill, they could hear the main branch of the Conejos River running. They immediately went to work. The horses were unloaded and fed, the saddles lined up along with the other gear that must be evenly loaded onto the two pack horses. After an hour of running around posing for photographs for Riley, they started to load the gear. After the horses were saddled and the pack horses loaded, they pulled out their costumes, as Ronnie called them. With ceremony, each put on his worn and dirtied chaps, each strapped on his spurs with the ringing dowels, each pulled on his own well-worn hat. Bill had a white hat that dropped low down over his eyes; Riley a bowler with a turkey feather stuck in the band. Ronnie had a small-brimmed gambler's hat, he called it; and Frank a bulldog rolled straw hat.

With a holler, they started down a slight downgrade that led then over the river and onto the trail to Green Lake. Of all the years of packing in the wilderness, they liked Green Lake the best. In August, the meadows are crawling with elk eating the last weeks of green grass and surveying their domain. The lake is deep and cold, blown into existence eons ago when the mountain top blew. It holds large cut-throat trout when one can catch them. As the men forded the stream down from the valley, they heard the faint cry of the Narrow Gauge train as Matthew Crane pulled the whistle.

The time passed. The horses snorted and filled their lungs with the mountain air, straining against reins to nip at the lush, green grass. After three miles, they stopped. It was a traditional stop. Here the trail bends to begin its climb out of the valley floor. The South Fork of the Conejos tumbles by as it rushes off the mountain. Beyond them was the turmoil of life, here the sound of the stream, and the smell of the aspen and birch. Letting the horses graze, the men stood in a circle, held hands, and hollered in unison, "One more year, we fucked you one more year." Then they threw their hats into the air and sat down and lit up a joint.

Beginning here and now, there was no time — rain, bugs, the sound of chopping wood, horses, yes, but no time; no government, no gross receipts tax, no kids needing shoes, no truck or car needing its endless supply of money to keep it running, no electric bill, no gas bill, no doctor bill.

"Jesus God," Bill proclaimed, "how in the hell can we make it without the stress?"

Ronnie took a hit on the joint, "I don't know. Maybe if we invent a pill that gives people stress we'll make a fortune."

Riley stood and took several photographs.

"Don't you think that through the years you'd have enough pictures?" Frank asked.

Riley snapped the shutter, "Never, never enough. You guys stand over by those aspen and let me get another shot."

By evening, they would be by the lake. Along the way, they would see deer and elk sign, grouse, sparrows, jays, a few wild crows, and the remnants of coyote-killed sheep. They spoke little, noticing the trees and leaves and the relaxing sound of the forest.

Reaching the lake, they went to hiding spots and pulled out nails, grills, and their pine tent poles they had been cut years earlier. They immediately fell into the routine of setting the camp. The ridge pole was run through the wall tent. Nailed between two trees, the cross supports were wired into place. Bill put the wood stove in the tent and ran the stove pipe out the hole in the ceiling. As it grew dark, they all stumbled into camp laughing and joking with arms full of firewood. As the fire came to life, the Coleman lantern was lit. They all stood and passed a bottle of Bailey's Irish Cream. It was good, they were alive. The government had not sold off the mountain to Exxon and for a week the world would go on without them.

Lying in their sleeping bags, the Coleman out, each man held his own thoughts in the reflection of the fire from the stove. Ronnie thought about his kids and how maybe they would never see something like this; never see the woods free, never be able to go back far enough to leave people behind. His kids living in their world of video games and cars. Kids of LA, space kids.

Riley lay and thought of the first time they had come here. A phone call, a sadness for distant friends, people to mark time and lives with, people to fight the loneliness with.

Frank exhaled deeply. There were no thoughts in his mind. Just the sound of the fire and the quiet of the night that surrounded the tent.

Bill lay, and in his mind's eye he saw the old shuffling train engineer sitting in his house, the walls cracked and dirty, the windows caked with coal dust and grime. The old man was sitting, sipping coffee, smoking, uncaring, unfeeling, unremembering his past. "His past lives," Bill mumbled to himself. He rolled on his side, and he saw the train pulling up the hill, trailing dark clouds of smoke and steam. He saw people leaning out the window snapping pictures and pointing to the scenery. He saw little kids holding onto their mothers, saying they had to go to the bathroom. He saw fathers looking out, running through their minds younger days of reading books about the Rocky Mountains. In front, giving the engine steam, he saw Matthew Crane smiling, talking to the engine, coaxing her over the mountains one more time. As sleep overcame him, he saw the engineer as a young man, standing with a young blonde-haired lady beside him as he told her about the train, showing her the large pistons that drew power from the boiler and pushed the wheels forward.

In the morning, after a quick cup of coffee, the men walked towards the lake with their fishing poles in hand. Frank looked at the water, saw a trout jump, looked at his friends, and then turned and looked back down the trail.

"Cocksuckers," he yelled at the sky, "all of you kiss-ass, mother-fuckers, you can't get me here."

CHAPTER 6

Matthew Crane took a deep breath and opened the refrigerator door. Nothing had changed during the last thirty minutes when he had last opened the door. He shut the door, turned, walked, and sat down at the small wooden table. He hated nights like this, nights when sleep did not come alone in a house that held no memories or warmth. He looked at his watch. It was still hours before it was time to be with the train. The bars were closed, Grace would not be at the restaurant for several hours. Nobody to talk to or smile to. Old age was hell at times. He stood, walked, and looked out the window that faced directly towards the railroad tracks. His house stood not fifty feet from the tracks. The red caboose sat even with his door, then the seven passenger cars, then the engine. He stopped them this way every evening. Matthew looked at the darkened caboose, old and outdated, but fresh with its coat of new paint.

Wish somebody could paint me, he thought as he turned and walked slowly back to the bedroom to lay back down. There was a time, he thought, shutting his eyes but knowing that sleep would not come. At times like these, his thoughts drifted to when he was a boy.

When Matthew was a boy in Kansas, he would still be asleep when his father went off to work. But, he would hear the cry of the locomotive that took his dad from Tribune to Topeka and back. His father didn't have a glorious run, cattle and pigs, but it was still a train. From the day he was born, Matthew was taught trains. He knew the names of the engineers and firemen, the brakemen. He knew the routes, and the speeds at which the trains ran. When it was time for him to find work, it was natural for Matthew to join the railroad. When both his mother and father were killed in a fire, Matthew left Kansas, moved to Durango, Colorado, and became the chief engineer for the narrow gauge railroad that ran up and over the passes to Silverton and Ouray hauling out the gold and silver. It was different coming from the plains of western Kansas to the mountains of Colorado, and coming from the large engines of the long trains to the small narrow engines of the mountains. But, he loved the line. It was the most beautiful run in the country.

In Durango, he married a Colorado girl and had two children: Bill, who was killed in Vietnam, and James, who died in a car wreck in California, trying his best not to work for the railroad. Three weeks after James' death, his wife died in bed, without suffering, a lost and bewildered look on her face. A year later, the narrow gauge shut down and Matthew finished his railroad work in Texas. After retirement, he moved to New Mexico with its sun and warmth, and he grew old and lonely. Erasing the sound of the engines and the flashes of his family that appeared before his eyes, he was tough, not asking for anything, sitting, growing older, waiting to die.

With his retirement fund, he moved into an old folk's home and began to remember about life. This led to his job with the Chama train. When this happened, he discovered that he was the last narrow gauge man in the country. Matthew *was* the train, the train that beat all odds, ran slower than any train in the country, and went over the mountains to come back again. When Matthew drove the locomotive, there were only the trees and animals, the colors, ever changing colors, from day to day, and mountains dressed by the rain, by the blue sky, by fog. Every day was a different picture. When driving the locomotive, there was no time, just the sound and the heat from the firebox, the wheels grinding the metal, and the urge to live, to climb, to breathe, to look forward, always up and forward. Matthew felt like a dinosaur; but, it was good to be last. Somebody had to be last. Somebody had to carry on the tradition of it all, keep the memories alive. That was all that mattered in life, it was all one big memory, no sooner dead than already a memory.

Matthew knew that over the past few years he had stretched the truth a little with people. Telling wide-eyed youngsters about the bandits he had seen as a sprout on the train, he made up stories about how Bat Masterson would ride the train from Chama to Colorado because he had a certain little gal he visited once a year. There had been one child sitting with his young blue-eyed mother who would forever tell his friends about the man who drove the train that Butch Cassidy and the Sundance Kid robbed.

What the hell, Matthew thought. It was good, nobody was hurt, and it kept him warm inside. Those stories and Grace's lunches kept the cold from his heart.

He remembered when he had first ridden a train. For his birthday, his father had promised him that he could ride with him in the caboose. The night before his birthday, he had lain in bed and not slept, dressed and ready to go when his father knocked on the door. He remembered walking through the train yard in the dark, his father saying hello to strange men, identities lost in the shadows. He remembered falling over the hundreds of tracks that blended into one maze. But, what he most remembered was the smell and feel of the caboose as he put his hands around the rail and stepped up and into the car. It was an ageless smell, a smell of men and work. Sitting with his father as the train moved down the tracks, Matthew had never known such a feeling of freedom. The flat Kansas countryside went by in time with the steady clank of the wheels.

God, Matthew thought, so many years, it's almost a crime to remember your childhood. He rose from the bed, dressed, and walked from the house. It was no use to try and sleep, and the night was warm. He walked along the side of the train and sat down on the steps of one of the passenger cars. He was home here, next to the train.

Home like some people are with children and friends, not yet grown, out-dated, not yet a novelty from the past for people to see, finding glory only in oneself.

He would tell people, "This is no movie, this is real; do you understand, real."

Matthew believed that Americans didn't really know what was real anymore. If they saw it on TV it was real. If they didn't, then they ran home to turn on the TV and see if it was on. If it was on, then they could believe it. Matthew sat and touched the wooden step of the car. He saw in his mind's eye all the different people who had stopped here, and he wondered where they were now and how many of them remembered the train.

Matthew walked slowly back to the house. It would not be long now. He would make his coffee and wait until he knew Grace would be in the restaurant.

Sipping his coffee, it dawned on him what was bothering him, It was not being old, not being lonely. It was the train. The train was like him, filled with memories but nothing else. Nothing for the glor-ly, only tourists and old stories. The train needed something to be. Like Matthew, it needed something to live for.

Grace opened the back door of the restaurant and flipped on the control switch for the lights. Down the street a few dogs barked, and a diesel truck geared down for its trip through town. She liked the restauraunt in the morning. After all the lonely nights, it was good to come here and start the coffee machines and make Matthew's lunch. By 6:00 a.m., she would have everything in order and the people would begin to file in. The cook would be singing, the waitresses spilling coffee, and she would be ringing up the register.

Over the months, she had grown to look forward to the sound of Matthew's steady step coming through the door each morning, dependable Matthew. He was like the train he engineered, on time, stable. By no later than six each morning, he would be at the door, dressed the same, smiling as he talked, taking his lunch, and going off to the train. At times, she would want to close the restaurant and sit and talk to Matthew; but, she was always busy in the morning, turn-ing on the stoves, filling the sugar bowls and the salt and pepper shakers.

At first, she had just made his lunch. But, as time passed, she took her time and gave him choice cuts of meat on his sandwich, and the best slices of pie and cake. When it was her birthday, somehow

25

Matthew had found out, he brought her two lovely purple Columbines from the mountains. He stood, not talking, and handed them to her with his large, soiled hands. She pressed them between the pages of a book, and later taped them to her mirror.

Matthew walked into the restaurant before she had finished with his lunch. She noticed that he looked tired.

"Good morning," she said.

Matthew smiled and sat down at the counter as she went back to the kitchen to finish his lunch. A few moments later, handing him the lunch sack, their hands touched for a brief moment. A shock ran up Matthew's arm and he looked at Grace. Grace smiled shyly and began to wipe off counter with a damp rag.

"Have a good day, Matthew."

"You too, Grace."

As Matthew neared the door, Grace walked out from behind the counter. "Matthew," she spoke tentatively, "would you like to come to my house and eat dinner tonight?"

Matthew was silent for a moment before speaking, "Why, yes . . yes, I'd like that very much, Grace."

"Good," Grace answered, "about eight tonight. You should be back in plenty of time."

Matthew left the restaurant and walked toward the train. The trees by the river were starting to take color from the sun. He touched his hand where Grace's fingers had grazed it, and smiled.

CHAPTER 7

Bill lovingly rolled the trout in flour and placed it in the hot bacon grease. Everybody looked on as each trout began to turn brown.

"If nothing else, you cook the best trout in the West," Ronnie said with admiration.

Riley took a long hit on the joint and passed it to Bill, "Here, it will help your appetite."

Bill nodded his head from side to side. "No, not now. Enough is enough. That weed is too strong, I'm too old to be a zombie every day."

Riley laughed, "With a bag full of this shit, I could crawl into a lot of that young pussy in Colorado."

Ronnie looked at Riley, "I should tell you about some of the lawsuits that come up from people crawling into that young pussy, as you say."

"That reminds me," Bill butted in, as he turned the trout with a fork, "Adam was lying in the shade of a tree. God said, 'Well, Adam, what are you doing?' and Adam replied, 'Well, God, we discovered fucking.' God looked at Adam and answered, 'Well, that was to be expected. It's natural. By the way, where's Eve?' Adam answered, 'She's down by the river washing off.' God became disgusted and looked towards the river, 'Lord, now I'll never get that smell out of the fish'." Bill laughed harder than the rest, explaining, "I like that joke."

They piled their plates high with corn, instant potatoes, and trout. It was good to sit and eat with friends. Good to sit and tell jokes and laugh. After eating, they lolled around outside the tent and watched the sun go down. Back inside the tent, they had a toot, a number, and a shot of Bailey's Irish Cream. While the others talked, Bill was strangely silent. Ronnie noticed his quietness.

"What is it, Bill?"

Bill rubbed his head, "I dont' know. Or, I do know but it's vague. You guys wouldn't understand."

Riley laughed, "We'd understand better than your old lady."

Bill poured himself a cup of coffee and sat back down on his sleeping bag. "It's just how things are, I suppose, that bother me. It's these mountains and that little narrow gauge train."

Riley shook his head, "Now, it's me who's supposed to get despondent, not you."

Bill looked at Riley, "I know, but I've been sitting here, and looking at these mountains, and thinking about all the different things that have gone on up here, and knowing that we may be the last, or close to the last people who come here who don't want to cut it or dig it up or scrape it away. We just want to sit here and be with the trees and fish. But we know, deep down inside we know, all this has got to go; in time, it will all go. It will all go into some form of official business. Hell, the government right now is probably trying to figure out how to give the forest a social security number. And then there's that train, running up and over these peaks every day, a thing of the past. It's like us. It knows. I tell you that train knows it's all over. It knows the deer are numbered, the elk, and all the people who don't like what the government thinks they should think. Hippies are all over, beatniks, hunters, fishermen, all the self-sufficient things are all over. If it doesn't have concrete on it, it's over. If it can't be controlled, it's pushed into oblivion. If it's worth money, it's all over. And the thing that bothers me most is that we can't do anything about it."

"Yes you can," Ronnie broke in, "you can vote."

"Give me a break, vote, vote for what? It's all the same. Government runs on money, ore, lumber, minerals. That's money, nobody can change that, and because of that, freedom is over. All the people who really knew freedom are doomed. It's all over except the dreamers and that train. We know, we know, all of us, I tell you, we know."

Bill looked at each man carefully, "I have an idea, an idea that will give life to these mountains, give life to us, give life to that old train that is too stubborn to lay down and die. I have an idea they will write books about, and make movies about, and people will tell their kids about, for years."

"OK, OK, what is it?" Ronnie asked.

Bill stood up in the tent and spoke very low, "Let's rob the Narrow Gauge Railroad."

Ronnie choked on his coffee. Riley, who was trying to get the last hit off a roach micrometers long, inhaled the roach, and Frank stood up, paced out into the dark and pissed.

Coming back into the tent, he looked at Bill, "What did you say?"

"I said, dress up like the old outlaws and rob the Chama train."

"That's what I thought you said," Frank spoke, sitting back down. He flicked some dirt off his sleeping bag and said, "Sure, I'll help. count me in."

Having fully swallowed his coffee, Ronnie began to talk quickly, "You're nuts; both of you fuckers are nuts. That's grand larceny, don't you understand? That's jail time if you're caught."

Riley didn't speak, his full attention was focused on the blister that was beginning to form in the back of his throat.

"Don't you see?" Bill spoke directly to Ronnie, "There will be a time when the whole country will be like LA or 'Frisco or Salt Lake or Denver or New York. All the gas and exhaust and people will be everywhere. And now, from coast to coast, there's only one narrow gauge running. One little train that tells people, 'Yes, there was a West! There was a time when there was freedom.' And we would be the people to bring that to the ears of the country. Business would boom for the train, everybody would want to be robbed. They could go home to their little, safe, push-button, stop light-controlled world and tell their friends about the robbery and how they were part of the last Narrow Gauge train robbery in America. We'd wear dusters, and hats, and old guns filled with nothing but powder, and do it. Rob that little freedom-loving train. We can do it with nobody getting hurt. What do you say?''

Frank laughed, already seeing the train and the horses running beside it, shooting his gun filled with blanks, watching the kids pointing their fingers, thinking it was a staged part of the ride. Riley said nothing.

Ronnie shook his head, "You're nuts, man. I'm too old for that kind of shit. I come up here to be with my friends and get sane for a week, not to go back in time and become a train robber.''

Bill shrugged his shoulders, "You asked me what was wrong with me, I'm just telling you.''

Later, in the dark, Bill lay with his eyes open. He could see the train, the smoke billowing from its stack, stopped by the tracks, the engineer with his hands up. He could feel the branches whip by his face as they rode off with the watches, cash, and credit cards. They would return all the money and cards, of course. It was just the doing that mattered. He sat up, and looked at the lumps in the dark that were his friends in their sleeping bags.

"Somebody has to do it," he spoke. "You know how it is, strokes of genius come to several people at the same time. Those that act get the glory.''

"There's no glory in this, Bill,'' Ronnie answered.

"Glory only to us,'' Bill replied, "because we would know, only us.''

Ronnie sat up and looked at Bill. "It's all true what you say. Any sane man knows the world is changing. Soon, there'll be no room for freedom as we know it. But robbing a train won't change anything, Bill.''

"Yes, it will,'' Bill answered quietly. "It will change my life.''

From the back of the tent echoed Frank's last remark for the night, "Cocksuckers, somebody should do it just to fuck with the cocksuckers."

Riley rolled over, "Could you imagine Cronkite on the six o'clock news? 'Four masked men looking like the James Boys robbed the last Narrow Gauge Railroad of America today'."

Bill was in the lead as they let the horses pick their way carefully along the narrow rim trail that circled Green Lake. They were on their way to Trail Lake and, from there, down the other side of the Continental Divide to Chama Lake. Cresting the trail above Green Lake, they stopped the horses and turned to look down the thousand foot vertical drop they had just climbed. Below, the lake shimmered in the warm sun. The fir and spruce trees swayed with the never-ending mountain wind. Above the lake, they could see for hundreds of miles in either direction. Here, there were no towering pine trees or aspen. Here, only a few clumps of twisted pine and igneous rock dotted the landscape.

After two days in the wilderness the men were in tune with their surroundings. The first day was always spent getting in, setting up camp, everybody still a ball of nerves. Everybody except Frank, who lived in the mountains anyway. The second day, the fact began to settle in that, for a few days, there really was nothing anybody had to do. It was hard fighting the propaganda of a lifetime. On the third day, everybody was relaxed, slower, waking to the sound of the birds, the chatter of the squirrels, and able to take the time to listen. They had decided to pack a few items, take a twelve-mile ride to Chama Lake, spend the night, and ride back the next day. It was a trail they had never been on and, for Bill, it would take him close to the route of the Narrow Gauge train.

Frank turned and looked at Ronnie. Riley sat and clicked off photographs as fast as he could. Frank said nothing, did nothing, but his mind recorded the detail: the swaying of the trees in the distance, the slow circle of a hawk over five miles away. Bill reached into his pocket and pulled out a joint. Lighting it, he took a deep breath. To Bill, there was nothing like pot in the mountains. A few hits and one became in tune with the horse and saddle. The eyes began to pick out hiding birds and scurrying creatures. One looked deeper into the colors of the paintbrush, the daisies, asters, and hundreds of mountain flowers. Bill took another hit, passed the joint, and then turned his horse and started once more along the trail. He felt good, he was on top of the world. He looked around him, took several deep breaths, and thought, freedom might just be another word, but environment has a lot to do with it.

Ronnie rode watching the back of Bill's head. The riders were each in his own world, but a world connected by good friends. They rode in the aura of their friendship.

"My corner of sanity," Bill would say.

"My little world," Ronnie would say.

"A photograph of the inside of my mind," Riley would say.

"My own cocksucking space," Frank would say.

They rode across the flat expanse of rock and scrub and pine until the trail began to descend once again. Below, nestled in the corners of the mountain, rested Trail Lake. From a distance, they could see a few trout dimple the water. From Trail Lake, they would travel through tall, towering spruce and fir, ford unnamed streams filled with small darting brook trout, ride through large, green meadows, and enter dark, damp tunnels of trees. They would pass strings of beaver ponds surprising, at times, the beavers who splashed the water with their tails and disappeared under the cool, clear water. After five hours of riding, they came to the edge of a mountain and looked down upon Chama Lake. From this vantage point, they could see the eighteen miles into Chama and, in the far distance, they could see the small dark cloud of smoke that marked the progress of the little Narrow Gauge train. They stopped their horses beside each other and their forms were silhouetted against the blue sky behind them. Bill raised up in his saddle and watched the smoke clouds. He imagined the engineer and heard the wheels turn. For a moment, he felt like an old outlaw, sitting and watching, knowing a time of meeting would come. Then riding down out of the trees with guns blazing, jumping from the speeding horse onto the train, making the train stop and galloping off with the gold to disappear forever into the crevices of another mountain range. Bill looked over at Ronnie and back at the smoke.

"You know, leaving Chama the train climbs for over sixteen miles before it stops at Cumbres Pass. Along that route, it's barely moving, huffing and puffing to reach the top. From Cumbres Pass, it goes through several large meadows and then through the forest again until it drops down and into Colorado. After the stop at Cumbres Pass, that's where to rob it." Bill grinned and looked at the others.

31

Riley looked at Bill, took off his hat, and rubbed his head. The horse nibbled at the tall, succulent grass and above them a sparrow hawk circled around the sky. Riley put his hat back on, "It would be something to do, Bill, it really would."

Ronnie looked at the lake, up at the sky, at the trees, down once again at the lake, then spurred his horse down the trail shouting, "Last one by the lake cooks dinner."

As they neared the lake, Ronnie fell back and Riley raced to win. Bill came in last; but, he figured he was the best cook of the group anyway and would just as soon eat his own cooking.

Frank looked at the trio and laughed, "That's fun," he puffed, dismounting. His horse's sides heaved in and out, sweat covering his neck. Frank patted his horse, "You like it old fellow, you like it, too. At least you know you're still alive."

That evening, sitting around the open fire, Bill fried the six small trout. The coffee pot perked. In the distance, they all heard the cry of the whistle of the train as it started its descent into Chama. Bill flipped the trout while looking at all the hungry faces and laughed, "Looks like a fucking beer commercial. I ride all this way and all you have is trout."

Ronnie sipped his coffee and, in the dancing light of the fire, his eyes seemed to turn red and his features age. The hat on his head drooped, and the leather chaps reflected the rays of the fire. "It just might be possible to rob that train, it just might be possible."

Bill looked at each of the men for a brief moment, "See, there's still some life in us, still a little of the old cause."

In the morning, before heading back to the main camp, they explored the area. Looking at the map, they noticed trails that might reach the train tracks. By mid-afternoon on the way back to Green Lake, they all decided it must be done. Back in camp by dark, they ate a cold dinner and spent the rest of the evening discussing what they would need.

"Shit, this is just like the Army," Riley said, getting more and more engrossed.

"It's like a good criminal case," Ronnie added.

Being content with the idea, Bill said nothing. Frank sipped his Bailey's and spoke, "It's a true red, white and blue cocksucker."

CHAPTER 9

Grace busied herself in the kitchen. Outside her window the old cottonwood swayed with the evening breeze. Inside, the aroma of tortillas and taco meat filled the air. Because she worked at the restaurant, she normally didn't cook for herself. There always seemed to be enough to eat. But this evening she was cooking for Matthew. She had almost forgotten how much she enjoyed it. When her husband was alive, it seemed as if she was never out of the kitchen but that was many years ago. The truck he was driving had gone out of control during a snow storm; she didn't think of it much anymore.

Now, she spent her time at the restaurant and in front of the TV in the living room. Going from day to day, unchanging, praying and hoping she would die before she was unable to take care of herself. If anything in life frightened her, it was the possibility of living so long that she would have to go to a home. There was nobody to take care of her, no children, no living relatives except distant cousins. Distant enough so that when she died, everything would go to the church.

She felt alive today, more so than she had in months. She found herself whistling while she turned the tortillas in the grease. Only minutes earlier, she had heard the train whistle up the canyon and knew he would be there soon. The passenger cars would be unloading the crowds of tourists. The bars and the restaurant would fill up for awhile until the crowds rushed back to Santa Fe or Albuquerque.

She removed several tortillas from the grease, folded them, and put in the mixture of ground meat and spices. Already on the table sat shredded cheese, chopped onions, and tomatoes. She finished her tacos, placed them in a baking pan, and put them in the oven to stay warm. Leaving the kitchen, she went to her bedroom to change clothes and freshen up.

Matthew had not rushed the train down the mountain as he wanted. It had been a test of his self-control not to open the throttle just a little. The thought of Grace had been in his mind all day; so much so, that this had been the first day he didn't really see the mountains around him or communicate with his locomotive. It had been the longest day he could remember on the train. Each water stop to fill the boiler seemed to have taken years, unloading and loading the passengers seemed like a study in slow motion, and the familiar turns and twists of the track seemed eons apart. But, as the train came to rest back in town, he looked at his watch and realized that everything had taken the same amount of time it always did.

Once in the house, Matthew took a quick shower, scrubbed the grime from under his fingernails, combed his hair, put on a pair of blue trousers, a light blue shirt, and his only pair of shoes. When he was finished, he walked out the back door of his house and, in the fading light, picked several large yellow old Man of the Mountains. Holding them as gently as he could, he walked towards Grace's house. He felt light and happy.

Grace answered the door when he knocked and took the flowers he held out to her. She smiled and rushed around the kitchen putting them in a vase. Not telling him they made her sneeze, she tactfully placed them on the sill of an open kitchen window. Matthew sat down at the table and breathed deep the aroma of food.

"Smells delicious; a lot better than my feeble attempts at cooking."

"Like a beer, Matthew?"

"Thank you, please."

They sat and drank the Coors slowly.

"How are the mountains?"

"Mountains are fine, fall is coming quickly. Another couple of months and the train will be sitting in the roundhouse waiting for the snow to go away."

For a moment, Grace could see the sadness in Matthew's face but, he soon masked it. When the train didn't run, Matthew didn't either. He would be stuck in the house, trapped as bad as if he was in the old folk's home. He finished his beer and Grace stood to bring him another.

"No, no, thank you. I don't need another one. One is more than enough. Used to drink a lot; no need, just a way out. I need my mind more than ever now."

Grace sat back down and looked at his grizzled features. She wondered what his wife had been like. He seemed so big and tough, and yet so gentle and lost. So unlike her husband. He had loved drinking and fighting but, he was a worker, a man who never sat still. She could not imagine Matthew ever being a fighter.

"This is the first time I have seen you in anything but your overalls."

Matthew looked at his shirt and ran his finger along the crease in his trousers. "Different, isn't it?"

Grace stood from the table. "I hope you like tacos."

"I love them . . . even dream about them. But it's been months since I've eaten one."

Grace brought the plate of tacos to the table. They sat and ate in silence. She was amazed at his manners. Most men she knew who worked hard for a living were not the best on manners. Matthew finished his fourth taco and pushed himself away from the table. "Those were delicious, Grace."

Grace stood and went to put the coffee on the table. He watched her as she walked, she was slim for fifty-five years old. He looked at her hips and thought to himself, wish I was ten years younger. Maybe, just maybe.

Grace sat back down with the coffee pot. "I'm glad you came," she spoke. "It gets lonely eating alone."

Matthew lowered his voice. "It sure does, it's the worst part of it all."

After coffee, they went and sat on the porch. It was dark, but reflections from the street lights made the trees seem to move. Down the dirt street, several dogs barked, and a car radio echoed from around the corner. They sat and did not speak. It was comfortable, nice to be like many old couples. A lifetime of being, no need for words or gestures, both knowing, caring. When it was ten o'clock, Matthew stood.

"I'd better be going; train runs in the morning." He stepped close to Grace and touched her cheek as she looked up into his face. "Thank you for everything."

Grace watched him disappear into the darkness. Down the street the radio still blared, but the dogs were silent.

Back in his house, Matthew sat on the edge of the bed and ran his fingers through his beard. It was good to feel wanted. He lay down and closed his eyes and fell asleep.

Grace did the dishes and then moved the yellow flowers out onto the porch, sneezing as she did so. Back inside, she undressed slowly and set her alarm for five-thirty in the morning. Under the covers she could see his face, feel his hand on her cheek. She wished he was in with her, his arms around her as they drifted off to sleep.

CHAPTER 10

Ronnie rubbed his hands, Frank chewed on a toothpick, and Riley rubbed his chin as Bill talked. The four men sat around the maps of the wilderness and National Forest, exactly like a road map in that every trail within the boundaries of the wilderness was marked. Even with these maps, people get turned around and die in the wilderness each year.

"It's really better than we thought yesterday," Bill said, running his finger over the dotted trail they had taken the day before. "See, if we could hit the train right about here, we could then ride over here."

"The only thing wrong with that," Ronnie interjected, "is all the open ground we have to cover to get back to camp. I know your plan sounds good, but there are some rough spots."

Bill nodded his head. "What are the rough spots?"

"Well, for one, pitching a camp far away from the train is good. Four men fishing doesn't make us the four men who robbed the train. But getting back here is a problem, it's not like a hundred years ago. We have to beat planes and helicopters now. Also, when we leave the mountains, we're going to go through road blocks full of cops because the authorities will know that whoever robbed the train has to get out of the mountains. Everybody on the trail will know it was four men on horses."

"I didn't think about that," Bill said shaking his head slowly back and forth. "Shit, nothing's easy."

Riley and Frank snickered.

"So," Ronnie continued, "we have to have a plan with a masking effect."

"Sounds technical to me," Frank butted in.

Ronnie gave Frank a shitty look and went on, "We have to have a plan where they don't really know how many men there were. We'll have to have a way back to camp through the trees. And last, but not least, we'll have to get back to camp without a trail."

"Those old outlaws didn't have to work this hard," Riley announced. "They just stopped the train, shot a few people, took the money and went to another territory."

Looking at the map, Bill muttered, "Fucking government has even made it hard to rob a train."

The rest of the evening they sat around hashing over plan after plan, laughing, then choking, as they laughed so hard.

"Jesus Christ," Ronnie cut into the merriment, "we've already committed a crime by even talking about robbing the train."

Bill shook his head. "Conspiracy, I know."

Riley burped. "Fuck 'em if they can't take a joke."

Frank added his two cents worth. "If we are guilty of anything, it is failure to conspire."

The next day was the last day of the trip. They fished and spent more time away from each other. It was a day of reflection and thinking about old friends. They knew it was over, and everybody in their own way savored the day. They had made another year and it was good. But maybe it was their last.

The next morning after breakfast they broke camp, loaded up the gear, and started off the mountain. The mountain would go on without them. The ride down was much quicker than the ride up. The men saw the forest clearly. Saw it with uncluttered minds. They smelled the earth scent around them and, before they knew it, they were back at the trucks. Within an hour they were driving towards the Wagon Wheel bar.

As they drank beer and looked at the tits, a game plan was drawn up between toasts to another fishing trip and the downfall of the Chama train. It was decided that Ronnie would pick up four dusters in California, and Riley would buy four pistols and holsters in Denver. Bill would have special calling cards printed, and would also ride the train several times to scout the mission. Frank would write a song about the robbery. It was also decided that nobody could get hurt, and that everything would be returned. They would meet back at the bar on August 6th, the following year.

Bill stood up from the bar. "Well, I'm off. I'm happy to have made another year with you all." He shook hands with everybody and left.

Ronnie, Riley and Frank shook hands a few minutes later and were off. The ride back for each of them was solitary. It was like the end of Christmas and back to work.

Strange, Ronnie thought as he headed for LA, we do this once a year and have a great time. Three hundred sixty days out of the year we work our asses off, fight and claw to get somewhere, be somebody. It seems backward. We should have a good time three hundred sixty days out of the year and fight and claw the remaining days.

Within six hours Bill was home. The kids were sleeping. The

dogs were curled under the coffee table while the TV showed some euphoric view of life. His wife kissed him hello and went back to her TV while Bill unloaded his gear into the garage.

"We'll do it. By God, we'll rob that train," he muttered almost to himself. But, without the others, he did not have the conviction of the day before.

Riley drove non-stop to Denver. He had not been in the house more than fifteen minutes when the phone rang. "Linda, my dear," he answered. He shut his eyes as the girl on the other end of the line spoke. He couldn't wait to see her, twenty-four years old, five foot eight inches tall, and blonde with long, long legs. He could see her legs wrapped around his neck and his face buried in her clit. He hung up the phone and sat down on the sofa. Back to the real world, back to hunting pussy. He stood up from the sofa and headed for the shower.

Frank drove through the gate and bounced up the dirt driveway to the cabin. Inside, he hung his fishing gear and sat down. Looking out of the window he hummed a few bars. "A song, a song," he mused. He had to write a good song. It might be worth millions.

Two days later, Ronnie pulled into LA. It was still the sprawling, polluted monster it was when he left. He looked at the yellow sky, smelled the gas-saturated air, and shut his eyes trying to forget the mountains and the trees. It would do no good now, not until next year.

CHAPTER 11

Every night had been the same for Bill. He could not shake the dream that haunted him. The dream had started with a cloud of dust. There was no definition to the cloud. In the background, Bill could hear the drumming of horses' hooves and the curses and swearing of men as they spurred their mounts on. When it would seem like the horses were upon him, he would hear a shrill whistle from a train, and the sound of steam mixing with the pounding of hooves, and the cries of the men. Then a face would appear from the depths of the cloud. An old sad face that would move with the cloud until breaking into a large toothless smile, it would say, "Rob it, rob it."

At first, Bill would wake with a start. Now he just rolled over and prayed he could get back to sleep. But, deep down in his mind, he liked the dream.

They were eating breakfast when Bill broke the news to his wife. Two of the kids were complaining about eating oatmeal. One child was through pushing his oatmeal around and was heading for the living room to watch TV, the other was feeding his toast to the dog under the table. His wife sat in her bathrobe and slippers, greeting another day in her joyful manner.

"I have tickets for the Narrow Gauge Railroad. It's time we all did something together besides watch TV and eat." Bill looked at the mayhem around him. The kid feeding the dog looked up and shook his head as if his brains were spilling from his ear.

His wife sipped her coffee. "Sounds wonderful, what's the catch?"

"No catch, nothing, just a train ride."

His wife sat her coffee cup down, "When?"

"Thanksgiving."

She took a deep breath. "You know we can't go then, my folks are coming."

Bill shut his eyes. "God, I forgot." Then, as an afterthought, "Maybe they would like to go."

Sally, his wife, laughed. "You know how my folks hate the mountains. Anything that might even think of having snow is out for them."

Bill looked at the dog chewing on the last piece of toast. "Then I'll go. You all have enough people around here, nobody will need me during the day."

"Sure," Sally countered, "you've never gotten along with my folks anyway."

Bill stood from the table, leaned over, and kissed his wife while she was trying to pull her cheek away. "Off to the station, have fun here at the battle zone."

Driving to work, Bill felt relaxed. He didn't want to take her folks to the mountains anyway. He patted the briefcase on the seat next to him. Inside was every map he could find of the area the train ran through: geological survey maps, forest maps, road maps. Day after day, sitting, waiting for the fire alarm, he studied the maps. He was like an infantry captain in his dedication.

39

Bill felt bad. But not in the way he was supposed to. He had spent the evening saying all the right things to Sally's folks, played with the kids who were more interested in their grandparents than they were in him, and informed everybody that he could not be there for Thanksgiving Day. Sally was angry that he had gone through with it, her folks didn't care, and the kids were oblivious. What Bill felt bad about was feeling so good as he drove towards Chama. Lord, he loved the fall.

As one drives out of the pinon and juniper-studded desert plain, every color imaginable greets the eye. The scrub oaks rimming the hills are alive in reds and oranges, vast mountain sides are splashed in yellow aspen. Ducks and geese, heading south for the winter, fill the valleys as they dodge the endless line of shotguns waiting to put them on the dinner table. Wheat fields lay in light brown stubble, home to the rabbits and crows for the winter. It was good to breathe the cool, crisp air. Everybody seemed to be happier, busily getting ready for the onslaught of winter.

"Only skiers love snow," an old Mexican told Bill once. "Everybody else hates the shit."

Bill drove leisurely. He felt in his pocket for the stopwatch and patted his briefcase with its assortment of maps. By the time he got back home, the turkey would be bones, the kids asleep, and his wife and her parents would be discussing what should happen with the kids. They spent their lives making a game plan for their kids. Kids will be something. They will find something. That's how simple it is. Everybody was something. Right now, Bill wanted to be an outlaw. He laughed out loud thinking of the caper and thinking about his friends. They had all planned to live in the mountains and raise their families in the simple aspects of life. They had all planned never to grow up and be like their parents. It was easy to have that idea when one came from the middle class. They were all just game playing, all of them caught up in a dream. But even now, after all these years, Bill yearned for the mountains and the playing. It bothered him that he had given up so easily. He would see his children running and playing in town and try to see them in the mountains without the backdrop of city living. He would look at them again, and it was as though their brains were hooked into cable TV. It was like Frank said, "Shit-head kids, commercial brains."

When he arrived in Chama, the train was being boarded. People in down coats clambered aboard the little red passenger cars. Bill made his way to the last car, the one, he had found out through some primary investigation, that had the bathroom. He sat down in the last seat towards the rear of the car. Within minutes a man, dressed like an old-time conductor, stepped into the car and walked through taking tickets. Bill had counted the cars before getting on. There were seven. Judging by his car, which held thirty people, there must be two hundred people riding the train.

Matthew Crane pulled the whistle and the train lurched forward. Bill pushed the button on the stopwatch and looked out the window. He took his camera from the holder on his belt and advanced the film. He had five rolls that he planned to shoot.

The Narrow Gauge travels north out of Chama for about a mile before it turns and crosses the Chama River and climbs to its first stop at Cumbres Pass, to let the tourists get out and buy the normal assortment of trinkets at the rebuilt train depot. Whenever the train is here, it is in constant view of the highway. Cars stop, the people waving at the faceless people riding the train. The train has a magnetism that reaches out and touches everybody who comes in contact with it.

Bill stopped the stopwatch as soon as the train halted, checked the time, jotted it down in his small black notebook and reset the clock, pushing the start button before placing the watch back into his pocket. The ride was fun and relaxing, sitting there surrounded by the forest and humanity. He could not remember when he had seen so many people smiling. Maybe life was not as bleak as he pictured it at times. He stood and walked off the train. Walking quickly, he headed for the front and a look at the engine.

Bill stood back from the crowd milling aound Matthew. It made him smile watching the old man talk to the people and kids. It was the same old man he had seen the evening he had stumbled drunk out of the Wagon Wheel bar. Several small children were crawling around the locomotive, examining, touching, dreaming they were like Matthew; not knowing the fight they would have with money to be what they wanted to be. Matthew looked over the crowd and, for a moment, his and Bill's eyes met and locked. For a brief second, they were not two people but one. They both looked away at the same time.

The crowd thinned slightly, and Bill walked up to Matthew. "How fast does she go?" he asked.

Matthew rubbed his beard. "Not very fast on this next stretch. From here on for awhile it's all turning and twisting, up and down, until we clear Munga Pass. Then it's on the brake all the way. But maybe on a straightaway and the right coal she would do thirty-five."

Bill looked at the engine and back at Matthew. "Thank you, just wondering."

Sitting back down in his seat, Bill waved goodbye to several people who were standing by their cars. The train lurched and he reached in his pocket and took out the stopwatch. Jotting down the figure in his notebook, he reset the watch and pushed the start button.

From the Cumbres Pass stop, the train rolls along the edge of several peaks and meanders across small streams and the highway several times before it once again starts to climb. The second part of the climb is more severe than the first. The peaks around Munga Pass are steep and the tracks switch back and forth, gaining altitude with each cutback. Along this stretch, the train barely crawls along. When the train finally peaked out, Bill looked at the stopwatch and, after jotting down the time, reset it once again. The train seemed to exhale as it entered an area that was relatively flat. Here, along the Los Pinon river, the train stopped again. While the engine took on water and coal, the people lined up with trays to be served lunch from GI serving cans. Bill sat until everybody got off the cars. A few fishermen got off the train with their gear and headed for the river. They would catch the train on the way back. Bill took a map out of his briefcase and marked where they were.

Matthew stepped away from the train. It was a beautiful afternoon. The fall colors drew his attention away from the mountains, away from the crowds. He sat down on the grass and opened his lunch. He always felt like a little kid opening his lunch, wondering what Grace had put in it. He never cheated by peeking into the sack before lunch time. He felt like an old dog with a new bone.

People ate and lolled around for an hour until the conductor called, "All Aboard!" Then, they piled back in for the descent into Antonito. From the Chama side, the train leaves surrounded by cottonwood and fir, spruce, and aspen. Coming down the other side, the train goes back down through the various belts of vegetation to a flat, grass-covered plain. It is not a pretty place, cold in the winter, hot in the summer; but it is a reminder of the beauty one has just been through. All summer and fall, the scene replays day after day. Matthew and his train watch the seasons change from the greens to the browns, and to the snow white of winter.

Bill watched the scenery roll by the window. He had everything he wanted written down in his little black book. It had been a good trip. He looked at the people and wondered what they would be doing now if they had been robbed on the train. He snickered to himself, and looked at the back of the lady's head in front of him. He felt good. He hadn't felt this good in months.

The ride back to Albuquerque was uneventful. He had not even stopped at the Wagon Wheel for a beer and a quick glimpse of the tits. The tits would still be there. Saavedra wasn't going to die this year and, if he did die, the new owner wouldn't hire girls with no tits to change bar policy. Bill lit the cigarette hanging from his lips as the sun went down, and went back over every detail of the train ride.

CHAPTER 12

Frank Cummings looked out of his cabin window. The snow was at least a foot deep and still falling. "Well, you're finally here," he muttered to himself. Frank was not like the others of the group. He was not hemmed in and jailed by the city. Long ago, he had decided that his mind would rule his actons. So he lived and eked out a living on his high mountain farm. He grew blue corn, squash, and enough pot plants for a stake each year. He picked up a little change guiding hunters, but he never seemed to get repeat customers because he always tried to talk them out of their shots. It was a good life. Most people would think it was lonely but to Frank it wasn't lonely, it was a way of life. Freedom has its price, wanting to live one's life differently than most has its price. The one thing that Frank did not like about living in the mountains was the snow. Winter depressed him. He couldn't find any great enthusiasm for snowshoeing, his truck turned temperamental at the first sight of snow, his fingers were always cold and his nose always ran.

So, in the winter, Frank sat around and smoked pot and imagined that he was a famous songwriter. The one capitalistic, egotistical endeavor he would give all the freedom in the world for was to be a songwriter. The simple fact that after a winter of jotting down notes and words, he normally threw the work in the stove unsatisfied, kept him from beginning the dream. He had never learned that satisfaction has nothing to do with making a living. But, being single with little responsibility, it was easier for him to hold onto many simplistic ideas. Frank looked at the glistening snow and his mind's eye roamed over the little stuck-away farms on the mountain. Now, it was beautiful. Tomorrow it would mean stuck trucks and frozen water pipes. He took a long deep hit on the joint in his hand.

Five minutes later, Frank caught himself sitting, unmoving, unthinking, looking out the window. Digesting, Frank called it. He turned from the window, threw a log in the wood stove, and sat down at the table. Picking up a pencil, he jotted down this line: SOMEBODY ROBBED THE CHAMA TRAIN. Smiling, he looked at his words. It would take time but he would get it, their theme song. He hummed the words, stood up, and put his coat on. Chickens needed to be fed, and the horses given some hay. He stepped out into the snow. Far in the distance, a coyote howled. Frank looked over the white field, even with the snow it was better than town. Even with the cocksucking snow.

Ronnie Wild went over the briefs on his desk. He had his choice of a good-paying coke case, several minor pot charges, or a combination rape and asault. He decided the coke boys would pay more. The pot kids were being fucked around, and the state could cut the balls off the rapist if they wanted. He stood up from behind his large, very neat, oak desk and walked to the window. Looking out from his seventeenth floor office, he stared first up and then down the side of the buildings facing him. He took a deep breath and ran his hands through his hair. The past months had been good. Knowledge of his dope case wins had led to many people hiring him for their defense. He was charging outrageous fees, and had several young attorneys under him. Everything was prosperous.

But lately, he was tired, listless. Page after page of briefs went before his eyes. His wife had a new Cadillac, his kids needed nothing. He had added another Jag to his collection. It had been all well and good, caught up in the game playing of LA until an evening several weeks ago.

Ronnie had been looking through a stack of magazines as he sat waiting to see another attorney. In the back of a horse magazine, he noticed an ad for custom-made, exact duplicates of the long cloth dusters that the old cowboys used to wear. Used for protection against the rain, covers for gear, tents, and everything else imaginable in a cowboy's life, dusters were the mark of a true cowboy. The ad brought back to Ronnie the outrageous idea of the train robbery that he had all but forgotten. He tucked the magazine in his briefcase and went on with his day. That night, sitting in the sanctuary of his bathroom, he looked again at the ad. The next day, he sent the check for eight hundred dollars as payment for four of the dusters.

After a week of waiting, he began to look forward to the arrival of the mail each day. When they finally did arrive, he put the package in the trunk of his Mercedes and, in the privacy of his office, tried one on. As he looked at his image in the mirror, he had to laugh. The duster was perfect. With his hat, he could rival any of Hollywood's wild desperadoes. Once again, the mountains ruined him and he spent all his time dreaming of the train and his friends. They will love these, he chuckled to himself. He could hardly contain himself, thinking about their reactions upon seeing the dusters. Jesus God, he thought one night as he lay in bed with his hand around his wife's left breast, we're really going to rob that train.

Riley Page looked over the classroom of over 350 students. It took him several weeks to get the best looking girls in the front row. But, he had accomplished this and spent many hours eyeballing young legs, thighs, and cunts. To date, during his life, he had never enjoyed such a sexual fantasy land. During the school year, he had sold over twenty-five photographs to various magazines, and his new notoriety had the young girls slobbering. There wasn't a night that he couldn't choose from a bevy of beauties, all young and firm, all waiting for the wisdom of his older sexual years to bring them to the utmost of their capabilities. But, after weeks of sexual activity, he began to think about the train. It became so bad that he drove down to the Geological Survey and bought maps that he put on his wall. One time, he had grown so excited thinking about the train that he almost called Bill. But he refrained at the last moment, placing instead in his mind the picture of a young girl, spread-eagle across the bed, her eyes half-open and smiling as he began to kiss her navel. When this fantasy was over, he would once again go over the maps; it was unreal and mind-boggling. The little steam-spewing train was

45

beginning to take on more meaning than young pussy. Lord, it was true what his father had said, "After thirty-five, son, pussy is pussy, just a series of in and out, in and out."

It was after a wild romp with a young freshman that he first saw the pistols. They were perfect reproductions of the old 44/40's that the cowboys used to carry, large, dark-colored weapons with deep brown handles. It would be a financial strain, but he put four of them on layaway with four holsters. The guys would love them. The pistols looked like they were produced for the sole purpose of robbing a train.

CHAPTER 13

Matthew Crane sipped the coffee slowly as he watched the snow continue to fall outside the restaurant window. Since the last run of the train in late November, his days were spent sipping a lot of coffee. Each day was the same. He would look at the train resting with its coat of snow, push from his mind the many weeks before it would run again, and then walk to the restaurant and sip coffee. The only thing that made his days bearable was Grace. After their initial dinner, they were together a lot, never really talking seriously about much, never a mention of younger days or children, ex-wives or husbands. They found a caring and warmth in each other. At times, Matthew would look at her and try to picture her with young breasts. Then he would dream of laying her down on his bed. The fantasy wouldn't last long. Matthew didn't dwell on what could never happen. A dream could happen, but a wish for youth, never. They could make your face look younger, put plastic in a woman's breasts, but there was nothing on the market that could put lead in a man's pencil.

"The only thing my pecker's worth is dripping," he told some of the other old men who inhabited the restaurnt during the winter.

Grace walked over to the table where Matthew sat, and sat down. The lunch rush was over and there would be time to rest for awhile. "Pretty, isn't it?" she spoke.

"I suppose," Matthew somewhat agreed.

"No need to be grumpy. Your mood won't make the spring come quicker and get the old train running."

Matthew smiled at her. "No, I suppose not. But it sure gets old sitting and vegetating, trying not to think."

Grace touched his hand somewhat reassuringly. "It's life, Matthew, every day of it."

Matthew shrugged his shoulders. "I know you're right. I'm just acting like an old man."

Grace stood. "Come on over tonight," she said.

Matthew nodded. He sat for a few more minutes and watched the snow. It was beautiful. But, like everything, a paradox. He remembered when he was a boy and, one winter, how it snowed for days. After the storm broke, he and his brothers had gone outside and sledded down the hills in cardboard boxes. It had been beautiful. That evening, while eating dinner, his mother had talked about all the cattle that had frozen to death, and how many families might lose their farms because of it. That night in bed, he had felt alone, mystified. How could something be so peaceful, so beautiful, yet so harmful, so deadly? He never told anyone his feelings about this. But, there was never a phase of his life that was not touched by this question.

Matthew stood and put on his coat. Waving goodbye to Grace, he stepped out into the storm. For weeks the town had been covered with snow. Each new snow piling upon the other. At first, he tried to keep the train uncovered by sweeping it after each snow; but, he had finally given up and just let it pile up. Now the little train looked like one long snow creature with a great big eye. Matthew walked across the street and into his house. The gas heater kept it warm, but it did nothing for the drabness of the yellowed walls. He sat down at the table and folded his hands.

Too much time, he thought. Too little to do with so much time. He stood from the table and walked to the bed. He would rest awhile before cleaning up to go to Grace's house.

Grace was excited. For several weeks her mind had been in turmoil. At first, she didn't know what it was. Then she knew, and the knowledge both elated and shocked her. She was in love. Strange, being in love had rekindled feelings in her that she had forgotten, including sexual desires. She went to the library and found several books about human sexuality, and there was nothing that said old people couldn't do it. Then one morning on the Phil Donahue show, she saw old ladies and men talking about affairs and the joy they found in each other. Grace put it in her mind right then, she would get Matthew's clothes off.

Matthew woke troubled from his nap. "Jesus, what a dream," he murmured as he shook the haze from his mind. The train was stopped, and huge billows of steam rose around it as a man with a mask walked up to it, pointed a gun at the engine, and fired. The train began to get smaller and smaller until it completely disappeared. Matthew stood and walked to the kitchen. He didn't believe much in dreams; but, maybe the train was trying to tell him something. He put on a pot of coffee, walked to the bathroom, and took a bath.

Grace lay the black negligee on the bed and looked at it. It was a flimsy number, not kewpie doll, but long and flowing, showing enough without being cheap. She stepped out of her clothes and walked to the bathroom. Looking at her standing form in the mirror, she decided that what she saw wasn't bad. A little soft, but close to fifty-six, who could complain? Her breasts were firmer than a lot of women she knew. Imagining Matthew's hands, she ran her hands down her breasts and across her stomach. Tiny sparks of joy ran through her. It had been years, too many years. She stepped into her shower, and took her time lathering her body. After drying off, she dabbed perfume between her breasts and on the inside of her thighs. She put on the negligee. Over the negligee she put on a long, soft, blue robe. Standing back and looking at herself in the mirror, she was satisfied. She went to the living room, put another log on the fire, and lit several candles. Dimming the lights, she sat on the sofa to wait.

After his bath, Matthew looked into the mirror. He rubbed his beard and hair.

"Christ, you look old," he told himself. He filled the sink with hot water, took out the scissors, and began cutting his beard. "It's about time this thing came off. Maybe it'll help."

Within thirty minutes, Matthew had the beard off. He stood back from his reflection and smiled. He looked ten years younger. Laughing out loud, he splashed cologne on his face. As he put on his coat, he realized that he couldn't wait to see Grace.

48

When the doorbell rang, Grace moved across the room in two steps. When Matthew stepped in, she could not believe how good he looked. Matthew stood as they both gazed at each other, finding it hard to speak. Grace's perfume swam around Matthew's head.

Grace broke the silence. "You look wonderful."

Matthew stammered, "You're beautiful."

They sat on the sofa in silence. The soft light from the candles reflected around them. Matthew sat like a little boy on his first date until Grace slid over next to him and put her hand on his leg. She looked up into his blue eyes and, with her other hand, undid her robe. "Matthew," she spoke softly, "touch me."

Matthew looked at the low cut of her negligee and the way the material clung to her body. He started to speak when Grace's lips met his. They kissed, and he moved his hand down to her stomach. Grace began to move with his exploring fingers. Entwined with Grace's body, Matthew found it difficult to undress. Grace slipped from her negligee and Matthew found her breast with his mouth. The perfume from her cleavage swept around him. Her thighs came up to meet his. They merged into one, and slowly, carefully, fought Old Man Time once again. Afterwards, they both sat naked on the sofa. Grace ran her fingers down his stomach and began to massage him.

"Jesus," Matthew croaked, "the magic is working again."

This time, they stood and walked into the bedroom. It was good to be in a woman's bed, good to feel soft, perfumed flesh. Afterwards they slept and, for the first time, Grace was late for work. Matthew didn't leave her house. He spent the day whistling and reading the books that Grace had checked out of the library.

A week later, Matthew moved into Grace's house. He packed his few belongings, looked around his dank little home, and walked across the street with his suitcase. Several people in town found it amusing, some thought it outlandish, but most thought it wonderful. For Matthew and Grace, it was lovely and warm.

CHAPTER 14

By April, Bill was going crazy. Every night he tossed and turned, dreaming about the train and the mountains. Each evening was spent watching the news and weather report for the Chama area. When the day was warm up north, he was happy. When it was cold, he was depressed. He had gone over and over his figures from the train ride until the times between stops, and the times between certain areas on the track, were ingrained in his mind. Bill's biggest worry was that, by now, the others wouldn't want to rob the train. Maybe the mystique had worn off and fear had set in. He had decided that if nobody else wanted to do the job, then he would do it himself.

Sally had noticed the difference in Bill over the months. She didn't connect all the maps and figures scattered over his desk with anything other than the annual fishing trip. She did notice that he spent more time in the garage looking at his camping gear, and seemed to take more time with the horses. He also seemed to be less attentive to the children. With her, it was old hat. They could go for days without speaking. But with the kids, Bill had always seemed open, now his mind was elsewhere. Whenever she tried to make conversation pertaining to this distance, he would look at her with a strange expression in his eyes and smile. She also had not been able to figure out Bill's overnight infatuation with old Western movies. He had never liked Western movies with their galloping horses, Indians, sheriffs, and endless strings of train robberies.

Outwardly, Bill saw himself as acting the same; on the inside, he was in turmoil. There would be no rest for him until the train was robbed.

God, he thought one night as he looked in the bathroom mirror, that fucking train has a curse on me. It's like the son of a bitch has my mind.

Three days later, Bill drove to El Paso. Leaving his car on the American side, he walked over the international bridge. The Mexican printer smiled a toothy grin at Bill.

"It will be no problem. I will print 250 of these for you, senor. You may pick them up in the morning."

Bill turned to leave.

"Senor . . . if it is not rude, why do you need cards like these?"

Bill looked at the Mexican, but said nothing.

Riley Page moved across the dance floor with Delores, the latest of his young things, as he liked to call them. When he met her in the cafeteria, he thought she was twenty-one or twenty-two. But a week later, as he kissed down the bottom of her rib cage, she told him that she was only eighteen. For a moment, he felt a pang of fear spread through his body; but, as her thighs pushed up into his neck, he forgot his fear. The last weeks had been the fullest sexual weeks in Riley's life. Delores was game for anything, anytime, and any place; in the park, at the movie, on the floor, on the sofa, in the shower. For the first time in his life, Riley knew he was getting older. She had worn him out. His dick was sore, his stomach ached. Still, he had to try. It had been her idea to go dancing. After screwing twice, she wanted to go. Driving to the country and western bar, she had tried to massage him; but, the magic didn't work.

"Later," he told her. "I need time." Maybe even vitamins, he told himself.

On the dance floor, she continually dug her pelvis into his groin and, when they danced fast, she was like a caged animal released. After dancing, he drove her back to his house. After coming through the front door, Delores immediately took off her blouse and fell into his arms.

"Fuck my tits," she said, and she lay down on the sofa.

Riley looked at her, looked at her two gorgeous tits and began to laugh.

"I might want to. I might even be able to without giving myself a heart attack. But not tonight."

Delores sat up and looked at him angrily. "You're like all the rest, you can't keep up."

She stood, put her blouse back on, and stomped out of the house. Riley sat down and nodded his head. It was good, she was the best ever, one a pimp could make a fortune on. He lay down on the sofa, shut his eyes, and fell asleep.

Frank looked out at the mountains from his window. It was late April and spring was in the air. It would be a few months until the peaks cleared; but, already he could visualize the mountains green and covered with wild flowers. It was coming, the robbery, it was coming.

CHAPTER 15

Matthew moved briskly around the train. Already, the hyacinths were blooming in Chama, and most of the track was clear going up and over the passes. It would only be a matter of time before the run would start again. Each day, crews were busy greasing and preparing the passenger cars and locomotive.

To the people around him, Matthew seemed years younger. His clothes were cleaner and he had a much more "taken care of" look. Everyone knew that Grace had made all the difference. Matthew did too.

As the day warmed, Matthew began to check over the train. He touched her, patted her, talked to her. He had even gone so far as to name her Grace. But he didn't tell his real Grace this, she might not understand the correlation, and he didn't want to rock the boat. Matthew might be old, but he was no fool when it came to the fragile female ego. By the time the maintenance crews showed up to begin preparing the tracks and the train, Matthew was like a kid.

It wasn't until the weather began to break that Matthew started to have the dreams again. Each night's dream was different but each revolved around the train. Matthew knew that whatever the dreams were trying to tell him, it was no good, evil. He saw dark dust clouds with figures who rode horses, men in long dusters with bandanas around their faces. He told Grace about the dream one evening after they had made love.

She sat up and looked at him seriously.

"Whatever it is, something is trying to tell you something."

"I was afraid you'd say that. I'm going to buy a shotgun and take it with me on the train."

Grace was silent for a moment. "It couldn't hurt."

The next day, Matthew bought a used, double-barreled twelve-gauge shotgun and a box of shells. When he made the run, he would be ready.

With spring in full swing, Bill's dreams began again; train dreams. He would wake up in the morning after another dream and wish they would go away. It was mid-day when Bill received the let-

ter from Ronnie. Never before had they broken the rule of no cor-
respondence. At first, Bill thought that it was bad news. He opened
the letter with a throbbing heart; but, the letter said simply, ''The
train . . . the reason . . . the dream . . . for all the outlaws.''

High in the mountains, Frank planted his corn, squash, and few
pot plants.

In Denver, Riley enrolled in summer courses, and started to date
a lady his own age. At least they had something to talk about when
they finished making love.

Bill made plans to ride the train one more time, to double check
his figures and ideas. There were still several things to work out.

CHAPTER 16

It was a glorious day. The crowds stood around the train snapping
photographs and enjoying the mountain air. Matthew looked over the
gauges and glanced at the shotgun hanging by a strap from the coal
box. He pulled the cord and released the steam. The birch and aspen
were green, and clumps of wild iris dotted the hillside. The peaks
were still snow-covered and would remain so for many weeks.
Laughing children ran through the crowd playing cowboys and Indians. Grace watched from the restaurant across the street. She felt
warm watching Matthew as he talked to the people and pointed out
various things about the train. Grace loved him dearly. It was good to
feel wanted, to have somebody to come home to. The whistle blew
and the people began to board the train.

Bill sat in the back of the last car and pressed the button on his
stopwatch. Everything was the same. Time had stood still. The world
came closer to war, taxes were higher, herpes was an epidemic, big
cities still grew in their cloud of pollution, but the train was still the
same. He looked at the people and the children, and scanned the
boards and windows of the passenger car.

''Don't worry little train,'' he spoke softly, ''we'll bring you back
to life.''

Like the previous year, the train stopped at Cumbres Pass to take on water. The people piled out to buy trinkets from the store. Cars pulled off the highway and joined in the general merriment. Bill walked slowly along the train and looked at the mountains. The mountains looked different in the spring than in mid-summer or fall. Although there was a lot of mud, everything was greening, and a few flowers colored the meadow. It was fresh and invigorating. After another winter in town, it was like being released from prison. Bill's senses came alive, his lungs gulped the air. Going back to his place in the train, he came face to face with Matthew. Their eyes met and once more locked as if they shared some common bond. Suddenly, Bill felt uncomfortable; he turned and walked away.

As he sat back in the passenger car, he checked the time on his stopwatch. It was within seconds of the previous year. Everything was the same, even the conductor and his procedure for picking up the tickets. When the train stopped for lunch, Bill got in line and thought over all the small details of the ride.

From the time they pulled out of Chama until they stopped for lunch, the train was constantly climbing. It went through several meadows. But not until it reached the area of the Animas River did it enter a meadow that was large, over a mile long and a mile wide. The robbery would have to take place before they reached the large meadow.

It wasn't until Bill was sitting by the tracks eating his lunch that he noticed a new addition to the railroad. There was a motorized, open air, flat car leading the train. The crew was eating lunch. Bill stood and walked towards them. He saw that they were young college kids with a summer job. They grinned at him with wholesome smiles when he sat down on the car with them.

"Good job you boys have."

"You bet," they all agreed, "fresh air, mountains."

"What do you do, anyway?"

One of the college kids answered, "Nothing really, push rocks off the track, or cut up trees that may have fallen over the tracks."

Bill detected a glint in the kid's eyes. Smoke reefer, too, he thought to himself.

As he walked away from the flat car, he felt a sinking feeling in his heart. He passed the engine and noticed Matthew eating his lunch. The old man looked up and waved as Bill walked by, then he went back to eating his sandwich. Once back in the car, the train lurched to a start. Bill pushed the button on the stopwatch and stood up. He walked slowly through the car and across the catwalk that connected the cars. After walking through all seven cars, he checked his watch, turned, and made the walk back. People in all cars shared the same state of mind. Everyone was relaxed, taken over by the breathtaking scenery and the charm of the train. Sitting back down, Bill took a deep breath and, as a man in front of him snapped a photograph of an elk that stood by the tracks, he suddenly had the perfect idea. It was there, in front of him like a flash, a pure and simple stroke of genius. And when one seeks, one finds, he thought.

CHAPTER 17

Ronnie packed the car quickly. Two of the kids were away at camp, and his wife, who had already said goodbye, was out to a luncheon for lawyers' wives. Ronnie shook his head thinking about his wife. He wondered how a woman could get together with other women and talk about what their husbands did. He finished loading the car and stepped back to take one last look at the house. Driving down the freeway, his mind was already two days away, looking at the mountains. It was funny. During the year, he hated the idea of travelling anywhere; but, when it came time to take this trip, he was reborn. He stopped the car on the top of the last hill before the straightaway to Barstow. Below, the grey-green cloud of pollution spread through the LA basin. He wondered what his lungs looked like after months of living in the city.

Riley looked over the gear that he'd spread out on his living room floor and sipped a beer. He couldn't see any good photographs in the gear, but he knew there was a market somewhere for a picture of camping gear. During the past week, he had thought a lot about the robbery and had wondered what Bill's plan was. He would leave in the morning. Already he could see the green meadows, the profusion of wild flowers, and feel the taste of trout in his mouth. Looking back at the pile of gear, he saw the four pistols, and chuckled.

———————

For two weeks, Bill was a crazed man. He smoked pot endlessly and didn't sleep unless he'd tossed down two shots of Jim Beam. Sally had given up trying to communicate with him, wishing that he would go on his silly fishing trip and be out of the house. Bill packed and unpacked gear, brushed the horses, then brushed them again. He looked over his maps and the little black book that contained all the figures. Then, he went over it again. His idea burned holes in his mind, and he wanted to tell the others of his plan. He bought two grams of coke, most of which was B-12, and bought a large bag of Mexican weed. After all, he thought, what were a few good outlaws without a few drugs?

He greased the truck, changed the bearings on the trailer, and checked the saddles for repairs. It was more like going into the wilderness for a year, his wife decided, not a week. She had the idea that maybe she could talk him into taking a trip for a month. She knew that she loved Bill and, with all their differences, Bill loved her. It had been many years since they were hippies. She would never forget the night they met. There she was, out of an eastern college and travelling west in a bus. The bus had broken down, and Bill and Ronnie had stopped to help them. Before they all knew it, they were sitting in a log cabin eating mescaline and Bill was the most beautiful mountain man she had ever met. After three days of running around naked, they were married; she with daisies in her hair and he with a bell earring. At times, she wondered what she would tell the kids when they asked how they met; but, as of yet, the question had never arisen. Through the years, as each child was born, and they delved deeper and deeper into middle class America, she wondered how their ideas had changed so drastically.

Frank walked around his small pot patch and lovingly checked each plant. He had the fifty-five gallon drum filled with water and the small half-inch tubing running to each plant. From each tube, a small valve released a drop of water — one at a time, drip by drip — on each plant. Positive that they would be fine, he rounded up the horses and hooked the trailer to the truck. It didn't take Frank long to get ready to go to the mountains. Frank had racked his mind over the past months trying to write a song about the train robbery but, each time he thought he was onto something, it led nowhere. He loaded all his gear into the truck. He would leave in the afternoon.

From four different points, the men began their journey. Each was caught up in the same dream: fishing the mountains and robbing the train. After Bill kissed his wife goodbye and got into the truck, all he could see was the train. He didn't picture the mountains, the lakes or the tent, just the train and the old man engineer. As he pulled out onto the freeway that would take him to New Mexico 285, he began to relax. His mind was clear, filled with only the purpose in his thoughts.

Bill strode into the Wagon Wheel and was surprised to see that Ronnie was there before him. Ronnie was sipping a beer and talking to a petite blonde barmaid who, for some reason, had breasts that did not overfill her blouse. Ronnie didn't see Bill until he sat down beside him and then his face radiated a smile.

Looking at the girl, he spoke, "One for my friend, Sylvia."

As he watched Sylvia walk away, Bill was impressed with her pert, round butt. "I think Saavedra has changed his outlook on women."

The two drank their beer slowly and did not speak. The impact of another year settled over them. Ronnie motioned for two more beers.

"You know, we should all put a thousand dollars in a jar and the last one alive gets to keep it."

Bill looked seriously at Ronnie. "That could be considered gruesome."

"True," Ronnie agreed, "but what the hell?"

"How's life?" Bill asked.

"Bought another Jaguar. The law business is doing fine. The harder times get, the more people have to break the law, and the more they have to hire lawyers."

Bill chuckled. "That reminds me, do you know why sharks never bite attorneys?"

"No," Ronnie answered.

"Professional courtesy," Bill finished with a grin.

"Funny, funny," Ronnie faked annoyance."

"I brought a little better coke this time."

Ronnie shook his head. "Not for me, I quit all that stuff."

"Jesus, you've made the final phase away from the sixties."

"I guess, old bones, or whatever. Pot and coke leave me like Jell-o anymore."

Bill scratched his head. "I know what you mean. I've been smoking a lot of pot lately and getting nothing done. It doesn't make it unless you're a movie star or politician."

An hour passed. With a few more beers, Bill and Ronnie relaxed. The other barmaid came on shift and, true to form, she was amply endowed. "Jesus," said Bill, "Saavedra has one for the ass men and one for the tit men now."

Frank was next to arrive. The door barely closed behind him when he screamed, "Cocksuckers."

The barmaids didn't even look when all three men stood and hugged.

"Well, that's three of us," Frank spoke. "Now, if the photographer gets here, we made it again."

After that, Frank was his usual silent self, and Ronnie and Bill went off on some conversation about taxes. Since Frank had never paid taxes, he really didn't think about it.

It was late in the evening when Riley pulled in. Ronnie looked at him as he sat down. "Had to get one more quick piece before you left, huh?"

Riley looked offended. "Not anymore, guys, this year I found a woman my age. No more chasing that young tail around, no more playing the fool for me, no sir! This lady is just that, a lady. And, she has a job."

Frank looked amazed. "How did you do that? I've been trying to find one with a job for years."

Bill butted in. "Well, move out of the mountains where there are a few people and you might find one."

Frank sipped his beer. "No thanks. Isn't a woman in the world worth that, not for this kid."

Riley laughed, his eyes glued to the butt of the new barmaid.

By one in the morning, the men were sufficiently drunk to start the drive to the trail head, going through the same routine they did every year they started out. As Bill climbed into the truck, he saw the dark form of the railyard across the street. Not one word had been mentioned about the robbery, but everybody knew the time would come.

CHAPTER 18

Matthew Crane woke with a start. Grace sat up. "The dream again?"

Matthew rubbed his head and lay back down. "Jesus, it was different this time. The train was coming around a stand of aspen when there was a blinding light and the train disappeared."

Grace held Matthew's hand. "Well, no matter, you have the shotgun now. I really don't think it's much to worry about."

Matthew shut his eyes. "I don't worry, but it sure keeps me from getting a good night's rest."

The season had been the best that the train had ever had. Each day found the highways jammed with cars and people lined up to ride the Narrow Gauge. There was even the weekly contingent of Japanese. Several magazines had sent reporters to do articles on the train and, one Sunday, the owners had driven into town and given Matthew a raise. Matthew was wallowing in the spotlight once again.

Bill was the first up and out of the truck. The dew was just beginning to steam off the grass, and the horses were restless in the trailers. He let the horses out, and gave them each a wedge of alfalfa. By the time he was finished, the others were outside the trucks. Ronnie was starting a small fire to boil up some mountain coffee, and Riley was heading for the trees to water the ground. Bill smiled to himself as he watched his friends. Everyone was a little slower in the morning, bones creaking and the mind crying for its shot of caffeine. Around them the sky was blue. Not a cloud marred the mountain tops. The birds sang, and the echo of the river met their ears. Timeless, Ronnie thought, timeless.

Frank began to unload the gear from the back of the trucks. Bill stood, took deep breaths, and shut his eyes. Soon the fire caught, and the blackened pot was filled with water and a handful of coffee.

"Mountain coffee," Ronnie spoke with love in his voice. "The only place it's good is in the mountains. It has to be the rankest coffee in the world."

After the gear was unloaded, and while the horses were eating, the men stood by the fire and watched the water boil. Soon, they were laughing and sipping the dark brew.

"Lord, I'm ready for Green Lake," Riley announced.

"Not this year," Bill uttered, seizing the moment, "not if we're here for what I hope we're here for."

Riley looked at the group. "Are we serious?"

Ronnie nodded his head in agreement while Frank spat into the fire. Bill laughed and spoke.

"Serious as a heart attack."

"Well, then, where are we going?" Riley asked.

Bill pulled a map out of his back pocket and lay it on the ground. Pointing his finger to a small X he spoke, "Right here, gentlemen, right here we start to get serious."

An hour later, the horses were packed up and ready to go. For the first time, when the trail to Green Lake went straight, they veered off to the left and started across another mountain. It was a pleasant ride, unfamiliar, but it had the comfort of the forest. There was an abundance of squirrels who scampered and scolded as they rode past, and many grouse along a tiny stream that the men forded several times. It was a good change, good to see new country, new rock formations, new game trails. They were riding towards a lake that none of them had ever seen. After several hours, they stopped by a marker that designated the Continental Divide. They dismounted, and stood looking around them, feeling small and insignificant, fleeting like the breeze touching their faces. As they remounted, they could hear, far off and rolling with the valleys around them, the faint cry of the Narrow Gauge as it climbed towards Munga Pass. Bill followed the sound with his gaze and turned in the saddle to look at the others.

"She knows," he spoke to the mountains and to the spirits around them, the outlaws, the badmen, sheriffs and miners. "She's calling us, by God." He laughed and kicked his horse.

The bay mare trotted and the others followed suit. Kicking and hollering, they galloped across the top of the world, stopping only when the trail became too rocky. The fact that they were in the woods settled into their minds. There was no need to whisper, hide, no need to do what one didn't feel like doing. Bill gulped for air.

"Well, I guess it's time for a toot."

Even Ronnie tooted. Promises were made to be broken.

By three in the afternoon they had reached No Name Lake. By four, the tent was set up, and the horses turned out to enjoy the fresh mountain grass. All the gear was stowed, and they rushed around outside waiting to see who would be the first to get his fishing pole together and run to the lake to catch the first trout.

"Last trout cooks dinner," Frank yelled, taking off in a run.

As the day darkened, the four stood around the lake, casting out into the water. They were together, but apart. Lost, except for the sound of mosquitoes and the small ripple of trout around them. Page looked at the setting sun and at the silhouettes of his friends. Hard to believe there's a place in this world like this all the time. One seems to forget some of the nicer things of life in pursuit of what we have invented as "nice."

By seven, the trout were fried and eaten, and the men sat around drinking coffee. As they let the trout digest, Frank looked at Bill and spoke, "O.K., great white leader, what's the plan?"

Bill looked at each of them slowly, pulled a joint from his pocket, went to great lengths to assure that it wasn't broken before lighting it, and in a marijuana cloud, spelled out his plan as he pointed to the map and referred to the little black book with all the times and calculations.

When Bill and the joint were finished, everybody was silent. Only the persistent buzz of the mosquitoes trying to get into the tent interrupted the night. Riley rubbed his nose, Ronnie shut his eyes, and Frank looked at everyone and spoke.

"It will work, by God. The cocksucker will work." He stood up and said, "Bill, you were born a hundred years too late. You weren't called to life to be a fireman, you were called to the life of a train robber."

Bill puffed up like the proverbial cat with the canary. Within minutes, everybody was in agreement that it would work. Ronnie stood and went outside. Walking back into the woods where he had successfully hidden the duster box while they were unloading, he opened it and put on his duster. Tiptoeing back towards the tent, he burst through the flap with his bandana tied over his mouth hollering, "Stick 'em up."

Everyone jumped. "Jesus, you fucker," Bill choked. Then he noticed the floor-length, bone-button duster. "You didn't forget."

Ronnie laughed, ran outside, and brought in the other dusters. The rest put them on and looked at each other. They put the hats on their heads and the bandanas around their faces. Looking sinister, Riley pulled the 44/40 pistols with holsters out of his ditty bag. Everyone was silent as they strapped on the guns.

"I had a friend load us up some blanks," Riley said.

As they looked at each other, all realized that, for now, there was no other world; no U.S.A., no Russia, no South America, no war on drugs, war on crime, war on fat people, just four men in a tent in the middle of the wilderness who were trying to stay a little bit crazy.

"Beautiful," Bill spoke, "it's really beautiful."

Riley snapped a photograph, Ronnie reminded him to develop the film himself, and Frank stood with a stupid grin on his face and muttered, "cocksucker," to himself.

_____

Down the mountain, Matthew ran a patch through the barrels of his double-barreled 12-gauge shotgun while Grace turned the TV on to Johnny Carson.

CHAPTER 19

The next day, the four men spent the morning gathering wood for the woodstove. They wanted to make sure that they had enough, no matter what the weather, when they made it back to camp. Riley cleaned his camera and carefully checked all the buttons. All were strangely silent, going about the tasks of the camp in grim determination. Occasionally, one would have another idea or think of something else they might need. When that happened, it would be hashed over and added or discarded from the game plan. At the present rate, they figured they could rob the train within four days. By mid-afternoon, with the wood split and stacked, Bill and Riley took a ride. Planning not to be back at camp until the following afternoon, they took food and a tarp. Riley took his fold-up spin rod and ultra-light reel.

From the camp to No Name Lake, the trail bends south toward Chama Lake, a distance of three miles. From there, it is six miles to a meadow through which the railroad tracks run. By dark, they were at Chama Lake, sitting under the small tarp, poking the fire. The coffee boiled, sending small steam puffs into the cooling air. Bill looked at his map.

"I don't like to have to go this far to get back to camp, but I suppose it's best. If the weather is bad, this trail will be a bitch."

The trail from No Name Lake to Chama Lake is solid rock. Sitting on top of the world, only the hardiest grasses and lichens eke out an existence on the rock-strewn surface. For one week out of the year, blue and yellow flowers, no larger than pinheads, dot the small rock crevices. It is an area that is impossible to take a horse through by any other means except a trail.

Riley poured the coffee and Bill sipped it, his eyes staring into the fire. He sat the coffee cup down slowly and, with his toe, pushed a piece of charcoal out of the fire. Letting it cool, he rubbed his fingers over the charcoal, then examined the dark smudges on his fingers. He looked at Riley and smiled.

"Between us and the tracks, there are two rivers we have to ford."

Riley sipped his coffee. "True, nothing we can do about it."

Bill rubbed his chin. "What a break, what a break."

By eight, they were in their sleeping bags listening to the sounds of the dark. It was peaceful and years away from the real world.

Ronnie and Frank left the main camp at dawn and rode quickly to the bottom of the mountain. Turning out the horses, they disconnected one trailer and drove into Chama. They ate breakfast at the cafe, walked across the street, and bought two tickets for the train ride on the last car for three days away. The girl behind the counter, small pert breasts poking through her T-shirt, was in her early twenties. Frank was stunned. He stood staring at the girl.

The girl looked at Frank and cracked, "Like what you see?"

Frank removed his hat. "I'd love your phone number."

The girl looked at Frank coyly, and quickly wrote her number. When she handed the sheet of paper to Frank, he looked at it in disbelief.

"Jesus, you live in Chama!"

The girl laughed. "Been in the mountains long, cowboy?"

"Look at that," Frank spoke as he walked away from the window. "I got her number. Jesus, Ronnie, I'm in love, I can feel it! It's the first time."

Ronnie laughed. "The only thing you're in love with is what's under that T-shirt."

Frank shook his head, "No, not this time. Her eyes, it's her eyes.

Greenest eyes I've ever seen."

The two got back in the truck and, as they drove back to camp, Ronnie listed the virtues of the blonde and the profound changes it would make in Frank's life. After they returned to the camp and turned the horses out, Frank grew silent. As he started the fire in the stove, he looked at Ronnie.

"What if she's gone when we get back? All this for nothing, my chance of a lifetime gone."

It had him. Love had conquered even the king of cocksuckers.

Ronnie read a book while Frank sat, sipped his coffee, and replayed the face of the blonde in his mind. Maybe it was her hair, maybe the nose, body chemistry but whatever it was, it was love. And Frank was bothered by the fact she might be gone and he had never even asked her name.

By early morning, Bill and Riley had followed the trail down from Chama Lake, crossed the Chama River, cut over the mountain to Grouse Creek, and followed it until they hit the meadow with the railroad tracks. Following the tree line, they rode, not crossing into the meadow until the tracks once again entered the trees.

"Right here is where we can jump off," Bill said as he looked at the towering spruce and birch around them.

Riley looked at the tracks. After going through the meadow, they turned out of sight.

"I wonder if the flat car will be out of view?"

Just then, they heard the blast of the Narrow Gauge as it pulled out of the stop at Cumbres Pass. They rode back into the trees, jumped off, tied the horses, and ran to the edge of the meadow to hide in some low scrub oak. Within twenty minutes, the small railroad lead car with four men on board came speeding through the meadow and disappeared on the other side through the trees. The seven-car train appeared next. Bill felt his heart quicken as the engine neared the trees on the other side of the meadow. Riley looked at the concentration on Bill's face. When the train was out of sight, both men stood and remounted their horses.

"Well," Bill said, "let's get back to the other owl hoots."

Ronnie was still reading, and Frank, still dreaming of the young blonde with green eyes, had turned his attention to her pubic hair and thighs.

Riley walked into the tent. "Jesus Christ," he snorted as he looked at Frank, "you look like someone ripped off your pot plants."

Ronnie put his book down and looked at Riley. "Don't bother him, he fell in love while we were buying your tickets."

Bill sat down. "Well, it should be O.K., the trail is fine, a little long and open in spots but it's okay."

Riley started to go over his camera again, Ronnie went back to his book, Frank thought about blonde pussy, and Bill looked through his flies. Tomorrow he would do some fishing.

Matthew Crane stepped down from the train. It was a glorious August day. The mountains were never prettier than in August when the hillsides were filled with wildflowers that bloomed in profusion. The purple Columbine was the most majestic of all. Entire hillsides were covered with yellows, whites, blues, and purples; pestomens, old man of the mountains, daisies, and asters bloomed for their few weeks of glory. Matthew watched the crowds empty the wooden cars. He was in a melancholy mood today, he was feeling sad for the train. He didn't know why, he only knew he was sad.

He walked across the road, saying hello to many people as he walked. Grace was busy sweeping the house when he walked in. Matthew set his lunchbox down, opened the refrigerator, and got out a beer. The sun was touching the mountain, sending purple shadows down the valley.

He sat on the porch and started thinking about all the faces of the people he had seen in the last few years, all the different people, fat people, thin people, beautiful people, children of every shape and color. While he was thinking, he remembered, for some reason, a fairly tall, dark-haired man who had ridden the train once last year and once this year. Once, they had spoken. Once, the man had turned abruptly when their eyes met. Strange, Matthew thought, to single this one man out. There was nothing outstanding about the face, nothing to make one pull it out of the crowd. It was just a face, a man with a moustache, blue eyes, and dark hair. He sipped the beer and tried to pull the face into closer detail, each whisker, the bend of the moustache, the tiny scar on the chin that resulted from once shaving in a hurry in high school. Matthew finished the beer and noticed that it was dark. He heard Grace in the kitchen and stood. Strange thing to think about, Matthew mused, as he walked into the house.

Grace put tamales on the plates.

65

"Lord, Grace, you're going to turn me into a Mexican yet, eating all this Mexican food."

Grace snorted, "Want to eat corn? Live with someone from Iowa. Want to eat beans? Live with a Mexican." Grace smiled as she sat down, "Besides, it's good for your sex life."

CHAPTER 20

At night, the sounds of Chama are muffled. Only the bar noise on Main Street penetrates the shadows. During the summer, travelers stumble from bars and head for their motel rooms or trailers parked at the RV park on the edge of town. Cast in the shadows of the night, they walk by the Narrow Gauge train. Blanketed by several overhead lights to protect it from vandals, it looms as a dark, resting relic. Most people who see it at night are afraid to walk up to it. Like a silent, dark god from the past, it rests, powerless, yet awe-inspiring; waiting out the destruction of the seasons, and the people around it.

When Matthew lived by the track, many nights he would walk out to be with the train, to sit on the cold metal steps or walk through the small wooden passenger cars. After he moved in with Grace, he very seldom visited the train at night. Even with her history and time-encrusted steel, the train wasn't warm and feeling. It only gave what one wants. Much like a horse or dog, it lives and dies through a chain of masters. Lately though, Matthew had been drawn to the train at night. Sitting there silent amongst the buzz of the mosquitoes, the singing of the river frogs and crickets, the backdrop of the cottonwoods.

Matthew and Grace walked out of the house. Regardless of the fact that the Narrow Gauge had run season after season, Grace had never been on the train, nor had she even wished to. To her, the train was a large, dark object that left a big black cloud of smoke as it pulled out for the mountains, brought the tourist who ate at the restaurant and bought gas at the gas station, and made it possible for her to live more comfortably. Though she knew how important it was to Matthew, it was not a part of her life. It was just a thing, a thing like any other thing. But tonight, Matthew persuaded her to walk with him to look at the train. They walked slowly down the street and, as they grew closer to the train, Grace could feel Matthew grow distant. Like a sailor and the ocean, she thought to herself. With a man, there was always something to pull him from home. As they walked by the engine, Matthew looked at Grace.

"They brought this train here in the 1860s. Can you imagine the stories she could tell?"

"How do you know it's a woman?"

Matthew smiled. "She's moody. They brought her here and, when she came, all the wagonmasters who'd made a living going back and forth over the mountains were out of a job. They must have stood here laughing at first, thinking this dark hunk of steel couldn't out-pull their horses and mules. She sent them scurrying for other parts of the West, scurrying and cussing progress and time and the new order. But, like everything else, it happened to the train too. Pavement came, then the trucks. They came to push her back into the roundhouse to sit and rust and rot."

Grace watched Matthew in the dim light. He seemed wise when he talked about the train, wise and sad and full of time and history.

"You know a funny thing about this train? It was never robbed, successfully, that is. Oh, it was tried, you've seen the old pictures and there were other attempts. But, it was never robbed. Every train in the West was robbed at one time or another, but not this one."

They continued to walk, passing the rows of windows that encased the small passenger cars.

"Can you imagine the different people that rode in these cars and all the different dreams they had as they looked up into these mountains?" Matthew dropped his voice. "That's what's wrong now. Now, there's nothing new, nothing fresh, no place for people to go to be alone, no place to explore or run. That's why they love her so. That's why they line up and fill the insides of this old piece of antiquity. Because for a few hours they ride in the inside of history. For a few hours there's no modern world, no cares, just the rickety rolling of the train and the clank of the steel wheels."

Grace looked at the old passenger cars, then at the old man. For the first time, she really saw Matthew. Saw him not as her lover, not as her friend, not as something that took the cold from her heart; but, as an old man who could be sad and quiet like all old men. An old man filled with stories and life who was tied to an old train. An old man who, unlike the train, had nothing to bring him back from antiquity. Grace felt a wave of sadness and grief and love sweep through her. She looked at the train, then she looked at Matthew. She reached out, touched his face, turned, and touched the passenger car.

"You're like this train, you old goat."

Matthew looked at Grace, pulled her into his arms, and held her without speaking. They turned from the train, and listened to the noises coming from the Wagon Wheel bar down the street. Several laughing people walked out and walked by them, looking at neither the train nor the couple who slowly made their way back to the house, where they sat on the front porch listening to the night and the ghosts around them.

Grace felt a cold chill run through her body, and she rose to go to bed. Matthew sat and looked out into the darkness, thinking, but not thinking . . . dechipering life, but not deciphering it . . . dreaming of men and years and time and the futility of it all. He got up and walked into the house. Taking off his clothes and trying to be quiet, he got under the covers. Grace slid into his side and Matthew ran his hand down her naked back.

"Make love to me, old man. Make love to me and tell me there is a forever and a constant in our lives."

Matthew cupped her breast in his hand and thought only of the present.

In the morning, they ate breakfast slowly. Grace talked him into taking her on a picnic later in the month. She would ride the train, and they could eat out on the grass while the others ate lunch.

When Matthew got to the train, the boilers were building up steam, and the crowds were growing restless. He stood on the locomotive and waved his arm to the conductor standing by the last car.

"All aboard," the conductor yelled, and the people began to board.

Matthew pulled on the whistle and opened the throttle. From the restaurant, Grace heard the whistle and smiled. Matthew opened the throttle more and the train was off. He looked around the inside of the train and noticed that he'd forgotten his shotgun. He would remember it tomorrow.

CHAPTER 21

Bill was up before dawn. He started the Coleman and got the fire going in the sheepherder's stove. After pouring water into the coffee pot without adding more coffee, he sat down on his sleeping bag. The others didn't move. Looking through his fly collection again, he made sure that he hadn't left one behind. Satisfied, he poured himself a cup of coffee, and drank it standing by the flap of the tent as he watched the horizon turn a dull grey. He finished the coffee, tossed the grounds into the grass, turned the lantern off, and walked into the early dawn. Across the meadow, he could see several does and fawns blend into the trees. From the branches around him, the birds began to chirp and rustle. In the early reds of morning, he threaded his way to the edge of the lake through the trees and small springs that bubbled around him. As he picked out a small, #22 Coachmen, he watched several trout jump in the middle of the lake. By six-thirty, he had several small trout in his creel, and he could see Ronnie tossing spinners at the far end of the lake.

Bill loved moments like this in his life. Among all the insanity of modern day living, it was these few and scattered days standing by a trout lake that made it all bearable. He had long ago gotten over the stupidity of it, the non-purpose of it. He only knew that he enjoyed it, loved it, dreamed of it. Watching the sun come over the top of the mountains, he felt the rays instantly warm him. At the far end of the lake, Ronnie reeled in a jumping trout. Bill sat on a large rock, and concentrated on the tiny ripples that the wind began to make on the surface of the lake. He wondered how many men, from the old trappers and miners, to the new fishermen with rubber waders and graphite rods, had seen this lake. Lost in thought, he forgot about Ronnie until he heard his steps close by. Ronnie sat down on the ground and proudly displayed a deep-bodied seventeen inch cutthroat trout.

"Beautiful," Bill commented.

Ronnie looked at Bill and became serious. "Well, the day is getting close, the day after tomorrow."

Bill felt his stomach tighten. Now that the planning and the days of dreaming were over, it was close.

Ronnie continued, "Is it worth it, Bill? Does it really mean something to any of us to risk going to jail?"

Bill looked at the trout laying on the grass, looked at the edge of the lake, breathed deep the scent of the pine and spruce, and heard a wren flick through the trees.

"It's worth it. It's worth it for all the wrong reasons, I suppose. Remember when we all met here?"

"How can I forget?"

"We were all long-hairs, smoking pot, doing all those things that the government figured would undermine the country. They made us public enemy number one and we weren't doing anything. The only thing we were doing was not producing. We weren't swallowing the old crock of shit anymore. We didn't want to be lawyers, firemen, bankers. We didn't want to pay taxes or fight wars or do much of anything except live. And you know, everybody in this country who was red, white, and blue had something to hate. They hated us as they went off to work in factories, hated us as they merged oil companies and sent guns to the world, hated us as they reposessed old peoples' homes and let Social Security fall to pieces. We ran around in the woods, laughed, got high, and dreamed of a world that really wasn't. We weren't part of it, we were away from it. Then one day we all looked around and we were getting older, and it was hard to be hated, hard to explain that we didn't mean any harm."

Bill grew silent as he looked out across the lake.

"And slowly, we became what we are now. Slowly, we did what we didn't want to do, and made up reasons why we were doing it, until even we believed the reasons. We went out and bought our TVs and cars, our houses in line with all the other houses. We taught our kids everything our folks taught us, and we put ourselves back on the shelf. We sold out, Ronnie, you and me and Frank and Riley, we all sold out."

Ronnie looked at Bill. "It's all too big, Bill. The country, the world, the FBI, the CIA, the KKK, whatever, it's all too big. There's no frontier anymore, no place to load our belongings and your family and try for a new life, a different life. We're all trapped, every one of us."

"I know that. We're trapped like that train. That train knows. People looking for freedom and new worlds and new lives ride that train., People who could shoot a gun and settle their own affairs rode that train, the last real earth people."

"What do you mean?" Ronnie interrupted.

"Earth people. We're space people now. There's a frontier, a lifeless, cold, dark frontier, a frontier of stars and planets and space

70

travel. It's not like the earth. It knows that some fucker somewhere will push the button or drop the big one. There has to be a place for a few people to run to, a place up in the sky. But for us, there's only the earth, and there's no place left to run. There's no place where there aren't police, radios, TVs, taxes, somebody, something that has it all mapped and planned and deciphered. There's nobody around who just wants to live and, if there are, they can't live." Bill stood and pointed with his hand. "Look at all this — the trees, rocks, game trails; the country used to be like this wild, free and full of life's promises. Shit, this'll all be gone some day. This will be a zoo with a fence around it, and for five bucks a college student with green walking shorts and big tits will walk you around, and point out a pine tree, a spruce tree, a deer, and an elk. And everybody will look and snap their cameras and go home to the TV and wonder if it was real. You know, one night I saw that train, and that train talked to me. I could feel the coldness in its heart, the emptiness in its being. I know what it needed. We have to rob it, not because it will make us rich, and not because it will make us famous. We have to rob it because nobody else would do it. Nobody would think about it, there is no reason. It has to be done because it's there." Bill sat down and scratched his head. "It has to be done because I'm nuts."

Ronnie stood, cast out into the lake, and began to reel slowly.

"It's been twelve years now we've been coming up into these woods, not counting the two years we all lived in different stages of hippiedom or lostness or whatever you want to call it. In twelve years, since returning to California, I've built up a thriving law practice, have enough money to quit if I want to. I've fed my kids, clothed my wife, manicured my dogs, had several affairs traveling around the world, and all I really feel is pertinent is standing here fishing, looking at the sky, smelling the wilderness, and catching trout." Ronnie paused, then continued, "You know why I love this? Because, of everything else in the world, this is the most constant. It's just here, here to see and breathe and be. Here, not to conquer or plunder or gain but just be, life and air and space. Here, to let you think and be alone. I've thought of bringing my kids up here, but they'd have to leave their skate boards and video games behind. They'd worry about the dirt on their pants or faces. They'd worry about the rain. Besides, I guess I don't want to bring my kids here. They're not like me, I'm not like them. It's not wrong, but that's how it is. Every year gets us closer to the last year, the year when one of us won't be here. In time, there'll be only one of us to stand by this lake and look back through all the years and remember all the good times. Then he'll be gone too." Ronnie cast back into the water. "And that's how the train is, going, being, not asking, accepting and puffing through every day for another day, another month, another year, until it, too, will be nothing only a memory. I thought for a while. When you wanted to rob the train, I thought you were nuts. Regardless of my fear of jail, it's dumb, it's idiotic. But, the more I thought about it, the more it made sense in a crazy sort of way. The more it made sense, the more I could feel the excitement, the danger." Ronnie's rod bent violently with the strike of the fish. The large trout jumped and spit out the lure.

They cleaned the fish they had caught earlier and started back to camp. The day was clear and bright. In the meadow, the horses grazed peacefully, and the grey camp robbers flew around looking for tidbits.

Riley didn't move when he heard Bill get up. Later, after he had dozed off again, he awoke to the scuffling of Ronnie. When Ronnie left, he got up. As Riley was leaving the tent, Frank was in the process of getting up. As he walked through the door, Riley explained, "Just going off to think awhile."

Riley walked down the meadow away from the lake. The horses lifted their heads as he passed and immediately went back to grazing. He walked until he found a small rock outcropping that stood up from the floor of the meadow. Climbing up, he sat down. From here, he could see down the full extent of the meadow, over the tops of the trees that circled the meadow, to a mountain range that simmered on the horizon over a hundred miles away.

There were times in Riley's life when he felt overwhelmingly afraid. He would wake up to find that a cold, bone-gripping fear had overcome him while he slept. He didn't really know the cause, it was as if there were none. There had been times during the war when he was afraid; but, these feelings had haunted him since before the war. Whatever the reason or the cause, whenever they came over him, he had to be alone. He looked out. As he watched the winds kick and bend the grass, and gracefully push the tops of the trees to a from, he began to relax. Slowly, he let his mind go out to the trees and breezes, seeing in his mind's eye a hawk that rode the down drafts of the valley around him. Within a few moments he opened his eyes and, once again, he was on track. He might be on top of the world, but he hadn't left quite yet.

So, he sat and thought about the years and time and his friends and all the changes, and he thought about the train and the passengers. There was no proper reason to rob them. Bill was a mad man, he could rationalize anything. Ronnie was a disgruntled laywer, Frank, too much of a hippie to be a cowboy. But Riley, he knew he was nothing but a photographer. All he could see was an old photograph of himself, dressed as an outlaw, standing beside a train. He wanted to rob the train. Maybe he wanted to tell the world "Fuck You" for the war. Whatever it was, he wanted to do it. He stood and started back to camp. As he walked, he heard the laughter of his friends. It was good to be in the wilderness with one's friends.

Entering the tent he looked at Ronnie first. Ronnie looked at Frank. "Come on Frank," Ronnie coaxed. "Sing it. You were supposed to write the song, now sing it." Frank looked at each of the men as though trying to find somebody who would say, no, you don't have to sing your song. But all he saw were faces filled with anticipation. Frank took a deep breath and quelled the butterflies in his stomach. "Ok, ok I'll do it. But nobody can laugh; this song is serious, ok?" The three men nodded their heads in agreement. Frank stood up and first clearing his throat he sang in a clear strong voice.

> Somebody stole the soul of my mountain
> Somebody took the heart from my train
> Somebody's robbed all of the freedom
> Ain't no place to start over again . . .
>
> World's crazy about lovin' the bandit
> But only the bandit lives free
> Bandit's crazy about lovin' the mountain
> Little train's crazy for lovin' the likes of me
>
> So cry on little steam engine
> Cry for the free and the brave
> Tell all the run-down city slickers
> About old cowboys and their yesterdays
>
> Toot your whistle for the outlaw
> Toot your whistle for the free
> Toot your whistle for all that's gone
> And toot your whistle for me

And tomorrow when fate awaits you
And gunsmoke fills the air
Know that four men really love you
Four modern bandits really care.

Frank sat down. "I don't have a refrain for it. It's really not very good."

"Jesus," Ronnie murmured, "that's a hell of a song. I didn't know you had it in you."

Bill looked at Frank as though it was the first time he had truly seen his friend. "You should stop throwing your songs away, Frank." Riley hummed the melody.

Frank, more amazed than anyone else, reached into his ditty bag, brought out a bottle of Jack Daniels, and poured four shots into tin cups. The men raised their cups and clinked them together.

"To life, love, money, and the time to enjoy them all." They drank the shots and laughed.

Ronnie poured four more shots, "And to good friends and being crazy."

By seven in the evening, they were drunk. "Tomorrow, we rest," Bill said as he fell into his sleeping bag. "Tomorrow night, we'll pull out. Time for history."

CHAPTER 22

Late that same night each man, in a subdued mood, sat on his sleeping bag. Everybody was off in their own world. Riley looked at the men around him and remembered the feelings that had permeated the tents in Vietnam on nights before missions. Those times were holy times. Some men wrote letters home, others played cards, others sat in small groups drinking beer. It was always quiet, as though nobody wanted to make too loud a noise that would anger another. Some men lay on the bunks and stared into the brown canvas of the tent.

To Riley this evening had been almost like those he spent during the war. Everyone was close without comment, and a warmth, a brotherhood, filled the tent. Riley looked at each man and pondered the phenomena of the feelings that men held for other men. There was something enduring in men's relationships, traveling together through lost loves and hardships. What did women know about war and taxes? Riley supposed that men needed men like women needed women.

Bill sat, going over and over the map, checking, rechecking, triple checking and looking at his black book.

Ronnie looked like a young lieutenant, self-assured in many ways, yet lost and afraid in others. Bill as the top Sergeant, on top of it all, placating the enlisted men and officers, running the army, settling disputes. Frank was the everlasting E-5, never dreaming of being anything else, and unable to kiss ass to get ahead. A good man in a pinch, but more interested in being alone.

"Feels like I'm in a tent in Vietnam," Riley blurted out, breaking the silence.

Bill looked at Riley and shook his head, "Can't relate."

Frank took a sip from the Jack Daniels, burped, wiped his mouth, and proclaimed, "Fuck Vietnam, forget about that sorry cocksucker."

Riley laughed, "One thing about you, Frank, we can always count on you to state your mind."

Frank sat the bottle down. "You know . . . you know . . . what if . . . just what if, when we rob this train, we happen to fall into something worth a lot of money? You know, with a little money, we might want to keep some of it."

Bill shook his head and scowled. "There won't be any big money on this train. Credit cards mostly, nobody travels with money in this day and age only small cash, beer money. Shit, everybody's afraid to carry money on them, they might get robbed."

Ronnie stood and pumped up the lantern. "We send everything back."

Frank grunted disappointedly. "I figured that's what you'd say."

"What would you do?" Riley asked.

"I'd keep it. I'd keep it and fix up my truck, build another room on my cabin, and get a better tractor. You guys forget, I'm not a big city success story like you."

Riley laughed. "Could you imagine a hundred years ago, and a group of guys ride out of the woods and, for some reason, while they're charging a train, they go through a time warp and, when they actually rob the train, all they get is credit cards. No gold, no silver, nothing but credit cards, would they freak out!"

Bill nodded his head. "To tell you the truth, I can imagine it."

"Years ago, those old boys robbing these trains weren't like the robbers in the movies, you know, they were some tough hombres. They'd kill you dead for nothing."

Frank sipped his Jack Daniels. "Well, you can't say that about all of them. There had to be some guys that were like people today. Every generation had a certain group of people who were caught up in it all."

Bill lay back down on his sleeping bag and looked at the ceiling of the tent. "God, life would have been different back then. A man could just get up one day, saddle his horse, and ride off into the sunset. He could go build a cabin, fight Indians, pan gold, or rob trains." He sat up suddenly, "Uh-oh, starting to fall off into the good old days trap."

Ronnie raised his eyebrows. "Good old days, hell, I'd rather have the good old days according to the movies any day."

Bill stood and began to pace around the tent. "All right, do we all know what we're going to do?" Everyone nodded his head at once. "The trail is marked for Ronnie and Frank, don't forget the charcoal. After you've dropped us off in town, get back here. Don't be screwing around. That means try not to find that little blonde you fell in love with, Frank."

Frank sipped the bottle. "I'm over that one already. Last night I kissed every inch of her body, looked into the essence of her soul and decided I was nuts."

"When you see her again, you might change your mind."

At five the next morning, Bill got up, wrapped his spurs and pistol in the duster, and woke the rest of the group. Riley put his gear and his camera in his ditty bag. By six-thirty, they were on the trail; by ten, Frank had let them off in town and headed back toward the mountain. Bill rented a room under a fake name, and he and Riley sat down to wait for the next day. Riley turned on the TV and found that Donahue, as usual, was eating quiche.

Frank rode back to camp with the three horses. Frank and Ronnie readied the camp, took enough food for a few meals and, following Bill's map, rode off. An hour passed without the two men talking. When they stopped for a break, Ronnie looked at Frank.

"Well, I guess it's too late to call it off now."

76

Frank laughed. "Yeah, I guess it's too late."

Frank felt good inside, he was living out one of his fantasies. He was a twentieth-century outlaw.

Ronnie watched the countryside. It always amazed him to realize that while it was peaceful here, only hours in one direction or the other led to a real world that still went on. Factories belched poison, cars coughed, and living went on.

By dark, Bill and Riley were tired of staring at television. The motel room was driving them buggy. They had rehearsed their plan a few times, slipped out for a quick dinner, thumbed through the latest issue of *Playboy*, checking out the beaver shots.

In the morning, Bill and Riley rolled the pistols and camera and other gear in Riley's ditty bag and walked towards the train. With several minutes to go, people milled outside the cars; it was going to be a nice day.

"Jesus, there must be two hundred people," Riley announced.

Bill paled, "Christ, hold the train if you have to," and he started to run down the street. He ran to the hardware store, made his purchase and ran back to the train as Matthew was pulling the cord to the whistle. He clutched two burlap bags in his hands. "Need sacks for the booty," he exclaimed out of breath. Riley shook his head, "It's the little things that get you, could you imgaine robbing a train without something to hold the treasure in?"

—

By 10 a.m., after a restless night under a pine tree, Frank and Ronnie tethered the horses and began to rub charcoal all over them. They walked through the trees and stopped where the tracks entered the trees once again. Tying two horses, they mounted and rode along the tracks to the smaller meadows below and sat down to wait.

The whistle called out and the little train began to inch forward. Bill swallowed hard and looked at Riley. Riley was frightened, but did not show it. Within minutes the train was huffing up the mountain. Bill looked out the window, "Well, we have some time, we still have the stop at the pass and then we have to get into action." Bill stood and went back to the bathroom; coming back out he handed his ticket to the conductor. Down the aisle, sitting with his father, a young boy looked out the window. "Gee, Dad, will we see any cowboys and Indians?" The father smiled and glanced at the couple sitting beside him as if to say, "gullible kid," but instead he spoke. "We might, you never know what will happen in this neck of the woods, I hear there's still outlaws up here."

Frank and Ronnie sat and listened to the birds. They watched a robin bounce after earthworms and two squirrels scold each other over an acorn. Overhead clouds were beginning to build and it looked like an afternoon shower. They had already changed into their dusters and had the pistols and bandanas on. Looking at each other, they had to smile.

Sitting on the train, Riley felt funny. He hoped Frank and Ronnie were in position.

Frank and Ronnie were getting antsy. Ronnie shook his head, "I wonder if the old outlaws got nervous."

Frank rubbed his chin, "I imagine they did, they could get shot a lot easier than we could."

Ronnie thought about this for a moment and did not like his thoughts.

Bill looked at his watch, within ten minutes they would be at the pass. He felt his heart quicken and beads of perspiration form on his head. Riley looked at him, "Take it easy now, fearless leader. It will all be fine." Bill took several deep breaths, "You know, maybe this is really a crock and we should just jump off this thing at the meadow."

Riley looked at Bill and looked away without speaking.

In a few minutes Bill added, "I suppose you're right. After all, this . . . this is no way to feel."

CHAPTER 23

Matthew Crane had felt uneasy the evening before. It was a nagging feeling, something was wrong somewhere. It was impossible to tell Grace, what would one say, something is wrong, but what it is I don't know? He sat through four TV shows, drank two beers and could not shake the feeling. Grace went to bed early, finding nothing to stay up for. Matthew seemed somewhere on another planet and she could not seem to get him back to earth. After the news, Matthew looked into the bedroom and Grace was asleep. He slipped on a light jacket and decided to walk down to the Wagon Wheel.

The bar held a few cowboys, several tourists and the barmaids, one with the nice ass and the one with the big tits. Matthew sat at the bar next to the two cowboys. Both looked a him when he sat down and in a cowboy way smiled. Matthew ordered a draft and let the sounds of the bar sink into his brain. After drinking the beer, he knew this would not help his feelings of misgiving and he walked out. Overhead, the night was clear; the moon on the wane. The Milky Way shone like diamonds over the top of the mountains. He walked back to the house without looking sideways at the train. Back inside the house, Grace was still asleep. He undressed slowly and got into bed. Within minutes he was asleep, his mind being bombarded with fragments of dreams that left him restless and tired in the morning.

Walking to the train in the morning, he did not feel well. Checking over the gauges, he made sure the shotgun was there in the corner. Looking back from the engine he watched the milling people. He was about to turn his head when he saw a man running at the train with what looked like two gunnysacks. He watched the man and recognized him as having ridden the train before. He watched the man get into the last car. Matthew shook his head, felt puzzled, cleared his mind and looked back into the engine. Sitting behind the controls, he began to feel better and after blasting the whistle, he pulled the train out of the station. Feeling the familiar vibrations and the touch of the wind on his face, Matthew began to feel better, but he could not shake the picture of the man with the gunnysacks. He must love the train, he thought.

CHAPTER 24

Riding up towards Cumbres Pass, Matthew looked out over the August landscape; on all hillsides the wild flowers bloomed, bees buzzed, and all the mountain birds gorged on the insects. It was times like this Matthew would always think of all the years he had lived without Grace. All the loneliness he had been through. It made him want to be like summer once again in his life, alive and new. For the first time, Matthew looked at the engine around him and he thought maybe this would be his last year. He would hand his job over and he and Grace could go somewhere where it was warm all year long.

Bill felt the train begin to slow down for its stop at the pass. He looked at Riley. "We might as well get out and walk around, no need to sit here and get cramped. It's worth seeing."

After the train stopped, Riley went into the curio shop and bought several small pieces of junk and two postcards. Bill stepped out and stood by the car. From the engine siderail, Matthew stood and looked at the man by the last car. There was no doubt about it, he was the same man. Matthew stepped down from the engine and walked back towards the last car. Nearing Bill, he smiled and held out his hand. "Matthew Crane," he spoke.

Bill felt shocked, but concealed his alarm. "John Blaire," he stammered, taking the old man's hand.

Matthew looked at the man, "I've seen you on this train before."

Bill returned Matthew's stare. "I love this train, loved it for years, love it now, it helps me stay sane."

Matthew looked over Bill's head and at the mountains. "Know what you mean, it is a staff to me also, something, something I can't quite explain even to myself."

Bill smiled and Matthew noticed the wrinkles around his eyes. They were good eyes, men knew people by their eyes. Bill looked around, "Well, I guess I'll go find my friend, it's his first time on the train." Bill hurried away from the engineer and saw Riley standing by the Coke machine. "God damn engineer recognized me from riding the train this spring and last year."

Riley looked at BIll, "Shouldn't be any problem."

"I hope not, but still, it's no good."

Matthew walked back to the engine. Funny, he thought, John didn't have a camera. Everybody who rides the train has a camera. Ahead, the men on the flat car started out to check the track. Matthew stepped up into the engine and sounded the whistle. The people began to load up.

As the train gained speed, Bill checked his watch. They had a little over six minutes before they would begin. Up the mountain, hidden in the edge of the meadow, Ronnie and Frank finished rubbing down the bay horses with charcoal. Back on the train, Riley stood and walked to the bathroom carrying his bundle. Inside, he put on the duster, strapped on the pistol, attached his spurs and hung his bandana around his neck. Putting the automatic flash back on the camera, he rechecked everything. Bill waited a few minutes and went back to the bathroom. Knocking, Riley let him in. Bill put on his duster and pistol and spurs and checked his pocket for the cards he had printed in Mexico. He adjusted the bandana around his face as Riley pulled his over his nose and mouth and they stepped out of the bathroom together. Bill spoke loudly, "Ladies and gentlemen, guys and dolls, children and infants, this is a robbery."

He pulled the pistol from its holster and spun it around his finger, holding the bag in the other. The people turned and looked at him and the children in the car pointed and laughed, "Look at the outlaws, look at the cowboys."

Riley stepped forward and Bill continued to talk, "As we come to you, please drop your billfold into the sack, my fellow outlaw here will then take your photograph standing next to me; you will get a card commemorating this great deed. The card reads, 'Congratulations, you are a participant in the last Narrow Gauge train robbery.' At the lunch stop a few miles down the track, you will get your belongings back." Bill stepped up to a young couple who had been sitting in front of them, he pointed the pistol at them, the young man looked at his wife and laughed as he dropped his billfold into the sack. Bill stood between the two as Riley snapped the photograph. Bill handed the young man his official train robbery card. Just then, Ronnie and Frank appeared riding even with the last car, out of sight of the engineer. The people pointed and laughed and snapped pictures with their cameras. Bill and Riley went through the car quickly. After the first couple, everybody was jolly and in the mood for the robbery.

Finished with the car, Bill waved at the people as they left and walked across the catwalk to the next car. Entering the next car, the people were already forewarned by a child who had run ahead of them. The adults faked being startled and held their children, "Look, look, bandits, don't talk or they will kill us." The children squealed with delight. "Ladies and gentlemen," Bill began, "this is a robbery." A small boy ran up to Bill and tugged on his leg, "You going to rob me, Jesse, please?" Bill looked at the little boy and patted his head, "You bet, young'un," he growled. "I'm going to rob everybody." The child ran back to his parents. They started with the same procedure, Bill standing between or next to a person with the sack open while the man or woman dropped in a billfold or purse while Riley snapped the photograph. Going on to the next seat, Bill handed the people their robbery cards.

Frank and Ronnie rode even with each car as they advanced. Crossing the catwalk to the next car, Bill looked at his watch, they were doing fine, four more cars to go and one sack was already full. Ronnie was laughing watching the children point at him and fake shooting the outlaws.

While the robbery progressed, the four men in the yellow lead car were riding and smoking a joint as usual. Talking, they almost ran head on into a downed pine tree across the track. Slamming the brakes on, one immediately called back to the train on the C.B., "Slow her down, Matthew, bring her to a stop, tree down."

Bill felt the train begin to slow and looked at Riley's eyes. Both men tried to hide their alarm. "Okay, ladies and gentlemen, get your picture taken being robbed on the Chama train . . . smile real big now . . . that's it . . . cheese." By the time they were finished with the fourth car, the train was stopped. As they walked across the catwalk to the fifth car, Ronnie rode up to them. Bill shook his head, the other two horses were tied at the far meadow waiting for Bill and Riley to jump off. Before Ronnie could speak, the conductor came from the front car out onto the catwalk. He looked at the three men. Bill blurted, "Howdy, it's going real good, better than they planned."

"What?" the conductor asked, puzzled.

"The robbery, they love it, best idea the people in the home office have had in years."

The conductor shook his head, "A lot of things go on here without me knowing it. All I do is take tickets." He stepped around Bill and Riley and went into the other car to tell the passengers there would be a slight delay and not to worry. In the car, the people were buzzing with excitement, children were talking about the outlaws and young and old were laughing.

Bill took a deep breath and Riley followed him into the other car. Ronnie rode out to where Frank was sitting on his horse watching. Inside the car, everything went as before. There were several people on each car who did not want to participate and they were passed without a fuss. In the middle of the last car, the conductor caught up with them and happily stood beside a young, shapely girl with a tank top and had his picture taken smiling beside her and Bill. Stepping out of the car onto the catwalk, Bill struggled with the two sacks. Ronnie rode up to him, "I guess you're going to have to jump on the back." He motioned for Frank to ride over. Everybody looked nervously around.

Matthew Crane had sat in the engine and cheated, taking half of his sandwich. Setting the wrapper down on the engine, a gust of wind took the paper and blew it out of the car. Matthew, who hated litter, started to step down and get it when he saw several figures with long white dusters and bandanas on their faces. For a moment, all his dreams flashed in front of his mind. "So, this was it . . . it had to be." He reached over and picked up the shotgun. He crept to the other side of the engine and lowered himself down to the ground. Once on the ground, he made his way to the edge of the car and stood listening to the men talk. As he stepped around the corner, he brought the shotgun to stomach level.

Ronnie saw the old man and could not speak. Seeing the look in Ronnie's eyes, Riley turned. All color drained from his face. Bill turned slowly and looked at the old man and the shotgun pointed directly at him. "Good day, gentlemen," Matthew spoke, "Nice day for a train robbery, nice day for the brave to die." For what seemed like eternity, nobody moved, nobody spoke. Frank broke the spell by riding up and putting himself under the steady gaze of the shotgun. Looking at the shotgun, he mumbled, "Oh, shit!"

Matthew stepped over the catwalk and looked at the men. His eyes searched the eyes above the bandanas. When his gaze rested on Bill, he recognized the eyes. He knew this man, this was the man who had ridden the train twice. For a moment he did not speak and then he spoke slowly and deliberately. "Nice outfits you men have there, you all look real old-time . . . dusters, spurs, bandanas, even nice old pistols." Matthew looked directly into Bill's eyes. "I used to dream at being an outlaw, read all those Western books and all." He paused and chuckled, "You know, I've been having dreams about this, weird dreams, dreams for months about men like you . . ." Bill broke in, "Dreams about clouds and trains and noise." Matthew felt shocked. Bill grew weak in the knees. Was it possible to have the same dreams as another man? Matthew looked at the men unspeaking, looked at the mountains behind them, looked at the train, "I love this train, for different reasons than you, my friend," he spoke at Bill. He looked at the group and slowly lowered the shotgun. "You boys get out of here, it's not a good day for dying."

Bill moved immediately and jumped on the back of Ronnie's horse. Riley jumped on the back with Frank. Matthew watched as they rode along the track and out of sight. They rode as fast as they could to the meadow where they were supposed to have jumped off to get their horses. Stopping, they mounted their own horses and as they were riding into the trees, the yellow flat car motored by. One man stood and peered at them as they rode off.

Matthew walked back to the engine and crawled up the ladder. Placing the shotgun in the corner, he rubbed his head in amusement. He was still rubbing his head when the conductor walked up to the engine.

"See the outlaws, Matthew?"

"Sure did," Matthew replied, stifling a chuckle.

"Must have been good for the pasengers, they're still laughing and carrying on."

Matthew started to laugh. What began as a light chuckle evolved into a long, deep rumble. The conductor looked quizzically at Matthew's explosion of laughter.

"What's so funny?"

Matthew turned, the tears running down his face. "Wasn't any put-on friend . . . it was the real thing."

The conductor stood speechless, "Jesus, I had my picture taken with them." He then told Matthew how they had done it. As the story progressed, Matthew laughed harder and harder. "Matter of fact," the conductor finished as he handed Matthew a small calling card, "they gave me their card."

Matthew took the card and read it aloud. "You have been a participant in the last Narrow Gauge train robbery," and it was dated August, 1983. "Sons of bitches," he said, laughing under his breath, "I'd like to meet those boys again, they must be some kind of fun."

The yellow car pulled up the train and the four men got out.

"See the outlaws?" the conductor asked.

"Yeah," said one, "there were four of them on black horses headed into the mountains."

"Well, you'd better get on your little yellow car and make tracks for town. The Chama train has just been robbed."

"No shit?" one asked incredulously.

"No shit," Matthew echoed, holding his laughter.

The four men jumped on the flat car and headed for town. Matthew pulled the whistle on the engine and spoke.

"Well, let's get to the lunch stop and tell these people that they've really been robbed."

The engine coughed, sucked in the steam, and moved out. Matthew felt the wind touch his face; freedom, it's only freedom, he thought, freedom, and hope, and prayer, and all those other things that make this life worth living. He pulled the whistle cord three times, and pictured four men galloping across the mountains with their dusters flapping beihnd them, and their bandanas wrapped tightly around their faces.

CHAPTER 25

As the train gained speed for the last hill before the lunch break, Matthew felt alive. The little train seemed to fly over the hills. He heard fewer rattles, and it moved as if released from a heavy load. Even the conductor lost his first sense of shock and felt happy. Funny, he thought, we just got robbed and I feel happy. In all the cars, people were laughing and joking, showing each other the cards that the bandits had given them. The children pointed fingers at each other yelling, "Bang! Bang!"

Even after the conductor explained to the passengers that the Narrow Gauge had nothing to do with the robbery, the passengers weren't alarmed. At first, they were silent as they all looked at one another. Then, a man who was standing in the back of the crowd started to laugh. He was joined by another, and another, until all the passengers were laughing.

"No different than a carnival," one woman said. "Guess you pay for your excitement, guess we paid those four men."

Matthew, in his mind's eyes, could see the blue eyes of the one man who had robbed the train. He knew how long the grooves in the forehead were, he knew the shape of he face, the color of the hair. Strange, he thought, that he could have sent his friends and him to jail. But there was no need.

Matthew took his lunch sack out and sat down on the grass. Across the way, with its backdrop of pine and fir, ran the Los Pinos River. Over the tops of the mountains rolled small powder puff clouds. He reached into the sack and pulled out the remaining half of sandwich. Unrapping the half, he spoke out loud.

"Now the fun begins, gentlemen. Now it begins."

They rode south, away from the train. The plan was busted, the police would know everything, how many men and the number of horses. But, everything wasn't lost. Bill led them away from the train for about half a mile, then stopped in a large thicket of alder. The others seemed nervous, but said nothing. When he heard the train pull out, he led them down into a draw and followed a small creek upstream into the mountains. Bill turned in his saddle to look at the others. The four had unbuttoned their dusters so that they hung open. The sound of the water around them blocked any chance of talking. Surrounded by the sounds of the wilderness, they rode. Except for their own knowledge of the present, it could have been 1865. Bill turned and looked at the bulging bag of billfolds hanging from his saddlehorn. After all the months, the time dreaming, thinking about the robbery, he felt drained. They had done it. True, they had almost been shot and the plan had been altered, but they had pulled it off. Pulled it off like the old days. Jesse James would have been proud.

Bill sat up in the saddle, clenched his fist, and held it up in the air. The others saw his gesture from behind. They all smiled without looking at each other. Jesus Christ, thought Riley. Ronnie shook his head as he weighed the penalties of the crime. Frank smiled and muttered, "Cocksucker, we did it."

Sliding off into a river, they began to wash the charcoal off the horses. Remounting, they followed the river another mile, they went over a gravel bar, up a shale path, and found themselves on the top of the mountains. From here, it would take another four hours to get back to camp. But, it would be fine.

Bill reined his horse, moved off the side of the trail, and into a deep, dark stand of pine. The others followed. Once hidden, Bill dismounted and tied the horse. Ronnie wiped his forehead.

"Looks like we made it."

Bill felt uneasy. "I hope," he answered.

Riley tied his horse and took the camera out of the saddle bag. Taking the film out of the camera, he ran over to the edge of a drop-off that plummeted at least four hundred feet. He set the camera down at the edge of the precipice, smashed it with a large rock, and threw the pieces out into the sky where they fell to the bottom of the ravine. Half-way back to the others who were still hidden in the trees, he heard the whine of a helicopter. Riley darted quickly in the trees, and hid in a mass of twisted, decaying trunks. Bill was drinking from his canteen when he heard the helicopter. Before he could say a word, they all dove deeper into the thicket, burrowing under anything they could find to hide them. The noise screamed above them and, with their faces buried in the ground, they listened as it faded into the distance.

Everyone sat up, each listening to their hearts beating in their chests. Removing their dusters, hats, and bandanas, they ran over to a large stone. Grunting and groaning, they all raised it enough for Bill to place the garments underneath. They dropped the stone with relief, glad that there were no tell-tale signs it had ever been moved. Ronnie looked dejected. God, he thought, those were nice things. Going back to the horses, Bill wondered what to do with the pistols. He hated to throw them away, but he knew they must.

"Guess we should sit here until dark. Helicopter should be out of here then. You don't fly in the mountains at night."

As the sun set, the four men rose. It had been quiet waiting for the dusk, each man away in his own thoughts. By eight, they were passing Trail Lake. The men stood on a cliff above the lake and, one by one, threw their spurs, pistol, and holster far out into the lake. They listened for them to land in the middle of the lake.

Several hours later, they were back at camp with the fire blazing and the horses tethered. Bill sat and looked at the sack of billfolds. He rubbed his hands.

"Here we go," he gloated. Opening the sack, he pulled out a dark, black billfold. "And for the first booty, what do we have here?" he chuckled.

The men were giddy. It was over. They had done it. Bill opened the billfold to look at fifteen dollars and two rubbers.

"I know which one that was," he laughed, "the young blonde guy with the little girl in the T-shirt."

Riley nodded his head. "Can't forget that one. She smiled so pretty for the camera while she was holding your neck."

Bill laughed.

Ronnie looked at Riley. "You two guys in there rubbing all that young body while Frank and I are stuck riding back and forth like two idiots."

They all began to open the billfolds and look at the money. Within a few minutes, a silence fell on the tent. The four became one mind.

Frank looked at the money in the billfold he was holding. "Cocksucker," he said in disappointment, "guess I'm a cocksucker like all the rest . . . but, I'd sure like to keep this money."

They looked at each other. Four faces held the same guilty look. Then they smiled and proceeded to dump the money out of the billfolds into a pile. As the pile grew, the men began to laugh harder and harder. Riley began to separate the money into denominations. Soon he had nice, even stacks of bills. He began counting. Without speaking, the others watched. After twenty minutes, Riley sat the last bill down on the ground, his face pale.

"Twenty-seven thousand dollars," he whispered.

Bill choked, Frank laughed, and Ronnie shut his eyes. Each man was thinking the same thing, twenty-seven thousand dollars . . . grand theft . . . Lord!

Bill jumped up. "Jesus fuckin' Christ, we have to get rid of these billfolds. God, who would have guessed . . . that much money."

They threw the billfolds back into the sack.

"God, what are we going to do with them?"

Ronnie grabbed the sack. "I know, follow me."

Grabbing the flashlights, they walked into the night. The beams from the lights fround the trail, and they walked for several hundred yards until they came to a big pine that had been hit by lightning. Bill pointed it out to the others.

"Remember? There's a big hole in the middle of the pine. I pointed it out to you once . . . remember? Right below the hole is a big branch." They shone their flashlights up into the stark, barkless tree, and could see the hole and the branch.

"If we can get up there . . ." Bill continued. Frank looked at the tree and the spaces between the branches. He judged the distance to the hole to be about thirty feet.

"I can," said Frank, and he took the sack of empty billfolds and started up the tree.

With his long legs, it was an easy climb. He reached the hole and stuffed the bag down deep. Climbing halfway back down, he jumped the rest of the way. The men walked silently back to the tent. When they opened the flap, they held their breath. Neat piles of money greeted their arrival. All shook their heads, all simultaneously realizing that, in their rush to rid themselves of the evidence, they had overlooked the most incriminating evidence of all.

"Lord, bunch of crooks we are," Riley commented. He picked up a pile of money, looked at the others, and said, "Now, what do we do with this?"

They silently sat on their bunks. Finally, Ronnie spoke.

"We should bury it and get it next year. There's no need to try and get it off the mountain. We've already seen a helicopter, so we know the police are searching."

"Sounds good to me," Bill agreed.

Riley picked up two coffee cans, dumped their contents into plastic bags, and stuffed the money in. They all stood and walked into the dark. Then, as if on cue, they looked at the lake. Surrounding the lake was an expanse of igneous rock the size of a football field. Blown into creation when the lake was formed, its jagged and sharp edges made travel across it almost impossible by man or beast. Shining their lights before them, the men stumbled into the rocks. They counted steps, and memorized the shapes of the rocks they passed, until they came to several rocks that were set at such an angle that all they had to do was to put the cans down in the crevice and roll the rocks over the opening. All agreed on the location, and quickly rid themselves of the money. Back in the tent, Bill rolled a joint. As they passed it around, they all began to laugh.

"It's over," they said, "it's all over."

Riley began to brew a pot of coffee as it started to rain. Bill lay back on his sleeping bag, and began to relax. Perfect, even the weather was cooperating. By morning there would be no tracks, only mud.

CHAPTER 26

By the time the train had reached the bottom of the mountain, the news had spread like wildfire through the town. Police sirens blared, and ambulances sat ready. By the time the news reached the sheriff, what had begun as a robbery ended up being reported as robbery and double murder. After twenty minutes of chaos, the sheriff finally got the whole story from one of the passengers. The sheriff called the State Patrol who sent out a helicopter. After making a quick sweep of the area, the helicopter, finding nothing, returned for gas. Finding it too late in the day to make another sweep, it was decided that it would remain grounded until the next morning.

The State Patrol set out road blocks, one at the bottom of the mountain going south, and one going north. It was impossible to get out of the area. The Department of Fish and Game was alerted, and patrol cars drove as far as they could go on the dirt roads that led into the wilderness trail heads where they looked for anything suspicious. By the ten o'clock news, the local news agency had the story, and ran a quick blurb on how the Chama train had been robbed by four men looking like the James Gang. And ABC news reporter happened to be watching the Albuquerque news and phoned the story to ABC. By eleven o'clock, a news brief about the robbery appeared on the national news accompanied by promises of an update on the area and the status of the investigation.

By six in the morning, reporters were seen flying into Chama's small airport, and the restaurant was buzzing with activity. The victims of the robbery were busy talking to reporters as they basked in their new-found fame. Grace, who was running around giving everybody coffee, was exhausted and out of sorts. Matthew, on the other hand, told the reporters that he hadn't seen anything, and he didn't even know that anything was going on until it was all over.

The Mounted Patrol was called but when the rain started to fall, the State Police knew a search would be useless. There would be no trail to follow. After all, they couldn't go around rousting all the fishermen in the mountains without a reason.

At dawn the helicopter crew was drinking coffee after a quick breakfast of ham and eggs. By six-thirty, a captain from the State Patrol had briefed them on the circumstances of the robbery. There had been four men on four horses, the men wearing white dusters, Levis, and bandanas. Two men on horseback were wearing chaps and different hats. All that most of the people could really remember was the bowler that Riley wore on his head. Figures that had been gathered led authorities to estimate that twenty thousand dollars or more had been stolen. One of the men was taller than the others, and the two riding the horses were of medium height.

"Not too much to go on," one policeman said.

The captain sipped his coffee. "Not really, not much at all." He sat his cup on the table and began to chuckle.

"What is it, sir?" the pilot asked.

"Oh, nothing I suppose . . . just remembering when I was a kid. Years ago, when the little train hadn't run in years, it sat in the roundhouse gettin' rusty and old. Us kids used to go over and climb all over the cars and engine and pretend we were the James or Younger boys. You know, nobody ever wanted to be the good guys, everybody always wanted to be the robbers. Frankly," the captain said after a pause, "I really would hate to catch these guys." His face scanned the faces of the others, "There's crime everyday — murder, rape, larceny, dope deals, extortion, you name it. But how many train robberies have there been in the last years?" Everybody shook their heads. The captain continued.

"Listen, if you do happen to see these guys from the helicopter, when you land, try not to hurt anybody."

The captain stood and walked outside. From the restaurant, he could see the little train, and the camera crews from the national news agencies, each filming their story. Once more, he remembered when he was a child, the feeling of the train, and the fun they used to have playing good guys and bad guys. He shook his head and got into his patrol car. Smiling, he drove slowly past the train on his way out to relieve the boys on the road blocks. They'd be hungry by now.

Riley woke first and dressed quickly. He walked outside the tent, and watched the fog from the previous night's rain burn off the ground. He breathed deep and exhaled. It was so fresh, peaceful. It reminded him of the aftermath of a battle. After all the noise and excitement, there was a moment of calm and peace with the earth absorbing her scars.

The men separated and went to their favorite spots on the lake. Bill watched as they cast out into the water. He looked down into the clear, blue water, then moved his gaze first up and across the face of the rock, and down behind him into the trees. Two red-headed woodpeckers darted over the water. He took a deep breath and exhaled slowly.

It was good. He was alive and he had friends. Sitting down, he thought about the old man and the shotgun. The whys and why nots of the situation posed a question he would never answer. They should all be sitting in a jail cell by now, sitting and feeling like fools. He sat and thought about his dreams, all the dreams he had lived through the last year, dreams of trains and old men. Lord, life was funny, tragic, but also funny. Bill felt alive and young again. He had cast his line and was reeling in the silver spoon when he heard the helicopter. Within seconds, it came tearing over the rim of the mountain and circled the camp. They all looked up and watched as it came to rest a hundred yards from the tent. Bill was closest to camp and, slowly, each man walked to him. Then, they all walked toward the tent.

"Let me talk first," Bill said, "we've only been here, understand? Just the truth."

The police shut down the helicopter and stepped out. They looked at the wall tent and the horses.

"Nice tent," commented one, "wish I was up here fishing."

They saw the four men come out of the trees. Bill and Riley stopped in front of the tent while Ronnie went in. Frank began to rummage around in the wood pile, as Ronnie restarted the fire for coffee. Between the four of them, they had three nice trout. As the three officers advanced slowly on the party, they looked around. The horses weren't black, but there were four of them.

Bill asked, "Somebody lost?"

A younger officer shook his head. "No, just looking around."

"Well, since you're here, come on and have some coffee. Friend of mine is brewing it up. We're just getting ready to have some trout and eggs."

The officers smiled. It was good to get up in the mountains and sit down. They walked into the tent, sat down, and waited for the coffee to brew. As he was sitting in the tent, one of the officers looked around.

"Nice tent," he commented, "nice way to take a vacation."

Frank rummaged through his tackle box, found what he was looking for, and turned.

"This one, this one here," he said, holding up a small yellow lure, "this one will catch old Mossback."

The officers drank their coffee and the talk turned to fishing. None of the officers mentioned the train robbery, no need to tip their hand. After all, anyone could see that these boys had been fishing for the last few days.

"Well," one of the policemen said, as he got to his feet, "about time for us to get going. Suppose you men haven't seen anybody else around here lately?"

"Nope," Riley volunteered, not too quickly, "saw some others ride through a few days ago, said they were going to Blue Lake. Saw some people on the ridge, but never talked to them."

The four watched as the men walked to the helicopter and got in. Soon the engine roared, and they were off with the trees.

"Well, guess the cops are looking," Frank commented as he tied another lure on his line. "They can look all they want, this boy's goin' fishin'."

Ronnie rose to his feet. "Think I'll join you."

Riley lay down on his sleeping bag. "You all catch a lot. I've got a new trout recipe to try on you if we get a bunch."

Bill stepped out of the tent and looked up into the sky. No, he decided thoughtfully, the old outlaws sure didn't have to dodge helicopters.

At the road blocks on the outskirts of Chama, the police stopped and checked all the fishermen, but found nothing. Back in town, the camera crews slowly filtered back to the big cities. The passengers who'd been robbed grew tired of answering questions, and went home to watch themselves on the news. Across the country, people read and heard about the robbery. There were close-ups of the passengers, close-ups of the train, and brief run-downs on the history of the area. Within days, the railroad was swamped with phone calls for bookings. Even the foreign press got wind of the story and scattered it around Europe.

Matthew Crane sat and watched the news. He smiled to himself. This is it, boys, he thought, everything you wanted, the train, the mountain — they're famous. It's not just a little smoke-belching train anymore, it's something grand and alive. It's a link with our past, a remembrance of a simpler time. It's alive, alive for another few years before it slips back into antiquity once more. He watched Grace walk towards the kitchen.

"Have they caught them yet?" she asked as she slipped through the kitchen door.

"No," Matthew answered, "haven't caught them, and they won't. Police don't have enough money to keep it up for long, too many real crimes going on in the world."

The four men began breaking camp slowly. Once again, the tent came down and the gear was folded up. Soon, the horses were loaded and, as the four twentieth-century outlaws mounted up, they looked around. Simultaneously, their gaze fell first on the rock pile that held the money, then on the lightning scarred pine tree that held the

93

billfolds. They looked at each other. With smiles on their faces they started down the mountain.

It was a leisurely ride in the warm August day. As they reached the trucks, a police car drove slowly by, but didn't stop. They unloaded the gear, packed the trucks, and started the drive into town. The road block was down.

They parked in front of the Wagon Wheel and piled out. Riley ran toward the door yelling, "First round's on me."

Inside, the bar was vacant except for one cowboy and the two barmaids. The big-titted barmaid walked over to the table.

"Suppose you want to know about the robbery," she said before asking what they wanted.

Bill looked alarmed. "What robbery?"

"You mean you don't know?"

Ronnie shook his head.

"Well, the Chama train was robbed. Four men held it up and got away with over twenty thousand dollars."

"Jesus," Frank exclaimed, "what's the world coming to?"

The barmaid laughed. "I don't know, but it's been on TV and it's even been on the news in Europe. People all over the world got excited." The girl looked at the men. "What'll it be?"

"Four beers," Riley said.

She started to turn and walked away. In mid-stride, she stopped and turned to looked back at the group. "You know, the people who got robbed weren't even mad. They were showing off these funny little cards that the bandits had handed them and laughing . . . most money this bar's ever made, I swear. I've heard the train is even thinking about having some guys rob the train every time now, not really rob it, just make it look like a robbery."

Frank laughed. "I'd like that job. Who do you see about getting on?"

"I don't know," the barmaid replied as she walked away, "ask over at the station."

"Could you imagine," Frank whispered excitedly, "we robbed the train for real, and maybe we could get the job to rob the train for fun."

Ronnie snorted. "Nope, once is enough for this kid. Nothing seems worth it twice. It's still hard to believe we really did it."

The barmaid returned with the beers, set them on the table, turned, and walked away. Riley stood.

"A toast . . . to us . . . to the mountains . . . to the wilderness . . . to the train." The four men chugged the beers and motioned for the girl to come back.

As Riley was making the toast, Grace was taking a bath, and Matthew was sitting on the porch watching the sun dip slowly behind the mountains. The town was back to normal. It had been fun, but it was good to get back to being normal again. When the train was robbed, and the town invaded by press, it had seemed to Matthew that the whole world was in the sleepy town of Chama, New Mexico. Matthew stood to stretch his legs, and decided to take a walk to the bar. As he walked, he said hello to a few people who were walking down the street. The little train sat bathed in the deepening shadows. Upon entering the bar, Matthew immediately saw the four men who were sitting at the table in the corner.

Scanning the group, his eyes fell on the dark-haired man. He knew it was them. Quickly he sat down with his back toward the table. The barmaid came over to him.

"Beer, please," he said with a gleam in his eye, "and a round for the table in the corner." Matthew turned, and watched as the girl took the beers to the table. He watched their expressions as they looked first surprised, then astonished, when they recognized the face of the man behind the shotgun. Matthew stood, held up his beer, and looked at the men. Tipping the beer to his lips, he drained the glass, smiled at them, and walked slowly through the doors of the bar.

Bill watched the old man leave. There was nothing to say. He stood and walked to the bathroom. Sitting down on the john, he picked up an old issue of Arizona Magazine and rummaged through it. Turning to the middle, his eyes grew large and he began to laugh to himself. "God damn, God damn," he muttered, "I can't believe it, I really can't believe it." Coming back to the table, he sat down and everybody felt the change in him. "Oh, oh," Riley spoke, "you look the way you looked when you were telling us about the train needing to be robbed." Bill took the beer and sipped it. Setting it back down, the opened up the magazine. "Look here," he spoke softly, "look what's going on in Arizona." Everybody craned their necks to look at the photograph over the article. It was a picture of a stagecoach. "Look," Bill pointed, "they're starting a twenty-mile stagecoach run in Arizona." After a pause he added, "Somebody oughta rob that stagecoach."